About the author

Chris McNaught is a Canadian barrister, university lecturer, artist, and author. An inspirational return to his Lowlands heritage has produced *Dùn Phris*, his fourth novel. He is profoundly grateful that his 'cold case' pursuit through the dramatic region of Dumfries/Galloway was well-fuelled by *Criffel* ale and fine whisky.

For Chloe with best wishes!

Chris McNaught

DÙN PHRIS

A GATHERING

Chris McNaught

DÙN PHRIS

A GATHERING

Vanguard Press

A CIP catalogue record for this title is
available from the British Library.

ISBN 9781784656 49-2

*Vanguard Press is an imprint of
Pegasus Elliot MacKenzie Publishers Ltd.*
www.pegasuspublishers.com

First Published in 2020

**Vanguard Press
Sheraton House Castle Park
Cambridge England**

Printed & Bound in Great Britain

Dedication

Again, as always, for dear Liz, Alix, Nick, and Carrie

…and for my forbears who grace the sod of St. Michael's and South Parish Church, Dumfries.

PART I
A Call from the Bar

1

It was a stygian, late March morning when he quit Peaks Island off Maine's lower shore. No vibrant colours, no lifting hope; what his dour grandmother, a borders Scot, called a *dreich* day. The sky, sullen sea, and iced beaches had melded in slate grey, and as pathetic fallacy goes, it should have been a clear harbinger. It was the day James Kirkpatrick learned, first hand, how one's life can implode in an instant.

It began immediately after pulling his 1964 MG off the ferry into Portland and his law office, a clapboard, pillar and porch affair at the corner of Congress and the Eastern Promenade. The salt-and-sail prospect beyond the parkland dividing the Promenade from the harbour had lent visual solace to an otherwise bland criminal practice for eighteen years now – bland, except for a sensational recent murder.

Oscar Pinkham's file had proven user-unfriendly from the outset.

A 'difficult' eighteen-year-old student at a local expeditionary school, Pinkham had made it onto the previous fall's 'canoe 'n' hike' week in New Hampshire. Staff agreed a wilderness disconnect from iPad and cell might achieve wonders.

Early one morning, somewhere on Lake Winnipesaukee, Pinkham had burst from his tent, catapulted by the sound of his self-proclaimed 'girlfriend' emerging from the woods, screaming 'Rape, rape!' She was followed closely by a State conservation officer. Without further ado, Pinkham had yanked a hatchet from the adjacent woodpile and flung himself at the pursuer.

In mere seconds, the officer, insofar as his head was concerned, became twice the man he used to be. The avenging youth was duly charged with capital murder. And no twinge of remorse appeared, even after Pinkham's arrest compelled a return to his schizophrenic meds; worse, pretrial detention fostered a vexing twist on the traditional solicitor-client relationship.

Inmate wisdom had it, and James could not honestly deny it, that you stood a better chance of ultimate freedom, or at worst, a better existence, if you sat on Death Row, as opposed to serving 'LWOP', as Life Without Parole was called. The latter invariably translated into a protracted death-in-life, languishing without benefit of occupational programmes or diversion, effectively forgotten by society: *if he ain't ever comin' out, why waste tax dollars on 'rehab'?* A young person facing execution, however, routinely attracted hordes of interest groups, wrongful conviction crusaders, law-student societies, all anxious to right perceived injustice. Accordingly, the chamber – Texas aside – on balance, stayed lonely. Roll the dice, and you could walk. *All or nothin' bro', think about it…*

James fought a losing battle, even though aided by logistical fact. New Hampshire retained the death penalty

12

on its books, but in practice, hadn't killed anyone in decades. James urged Pinkham to push his medical condition, while pressing a classic 'crime of passion – misplaced vengeance' scenario, hanging in for a plea to something less than capital murder.

Pinkham dug his own grave, deeply, against James' strategy. At trial, he was persistently obnoxious, an uncooperative, self-destructive witness. In lieu of crying out for empathy with the emotional reflex, he repeated at every opportunity how coolly he'd carried out his 'duty', urging the jury to consider his selection of the hatchet as an 'aggravating circumstance'. The twelve angry citizens obliged, to the extent of finding Pinkham guilty of capital murder.

At sentence, he shunned James and moved to exercise the rare privilege of 'allocution': addressing the jury without counsel. The jury listened, aghast, as his client pleaded for the death penalty, then voted for LWOP.

A keen young public defender filed bizarre applications to first the State, then US Supreme Court, the doomed premise being a 'constitutional' challenge: if Pinkham had the right to 'life, liberty,' etc., then in a novel spin on the 'right to die' movement, he surely had the right to *relinquish* that right of his own will, via capital punishment, especially if applicable State law technically allowed such.

On reflection, the sole enjoyable jury moment for the long-suffering James came when he casually pronounced 'Lake Winnipesaukee' like a true native.

This morning, the predictable denial from the Washington bench was posted on its website for the world to see, and with it, James felt finally rid of Oscar Pinkham – until, his first café Sumatra 'with a double shot in the dark' in hand, he opened the snail mail. A large cream envelope from Concord bore a succinct message under the embossed letterhead of the 'New Hampshire Bar Association, *Equal Justice Under Law*':

Dear Mr Kirkpatrick,

A Complaint has been filed with the Association by your former client, Oscar B. Pinkham.

The Complaint alleges 'professional incompetence'. Particulars of the Complaint are set out both in Mr Pinkham's original letter to the Association, as well as in the formal Complaint (copies of both enclosed).

Please file a written response, in triplicate, within three weeks. The Association takes all complaints against its members seriously, and we urge you to give this matter your prompt and utmost consideration…

What James 'gave' it was a coffee cup flung against the wall and a middle finger stabbed in the air, followed by twenty minutes of melodramatic pacing out on the balcony, snow and weather notwithstanding.

'… Kirkpatrick ignored my instructions and wishes, made me look like a crazy in front of the jury, and forced me to speak to them without assistance…'

It wasn't that James expected gratitude for miraculously downplaying the minor fact the conservation officer was not the heinous culprit, but the *rescuer* of the fair damsel, from a local fisherman who couldn't believe his luck. What galled was that an actual attorney had affixed his reputation to the complaint on Pinkham's behalf. One, 'Alexander Toussaint Dahlgren III'. Either the South had risen again, or some sleazoid had managed to get reinstated; James imagined a shabby character, played by Hackman or Pacino, ensconced in a Days Inn, glued to *Columbo* re-runs, waiting for adulation.

Tendrils of snow wafted from the branches of the abutting maple failed to cool his enflamed cheeks. James was not intemperate, a cool veteran of the legal trenches, a believer, despite much evidence to the contrary, in the predominance of good in most, *but...*

He had a fleeting sense his funk might herald something more profound, but for the moment, the bracing ether gradually sapped the venom and he looked for a positive sign. Maybe the complaint marked a tipping point, a hint – an *invitation*? After all, what was he doing here in his early forties on this upscale shore, schlepping out a supposedly 'professional calling'? Spending 90% of his waking hours defending cranky baby boomers, entitled brats and life's violent losers. Where was his once-curious mind these days, his happy recourse to the glorious shelves of Greece and Rome? When had he last been *inspired* for Christ's sake?

Down on the Promenade, a huge bus thundered by, branded with political slogans under the sneering visage of a wannabe candidate coiffed in a yellow pompadour challenging Marie Antoinette. James suddenly felt rootless. How *was* it to be 'American' these days? 'Give me your tired, your poor – and we'll *deport* them! We'll be great again, *behind a wall!'* In 2016, in a *web*-world? He peered wistfully through the leafless border across the way in the general direction of the winter berth of his trusty sloop, *The Rigged Jury*. He tried to conjure the smell of canvas on a summer tack. Come next season, maybe he'd simply launch and hold easterly, outrun the antediluvian sludge…

Winter wishes.

James went back in and puttered aimlessly at some minor files for an hour or so, then told Angie to knock off early, closed up, and drove over to the mid-afternoon ferry, grabbing an ugly cheeseburger from *Crabby Anne's* to absorb his bile.

Three weeks to respond – *assuming* he…

***

"Charlie?"

James' better half was born 'Charlotte', her sibling, 'Charles'; she'd left him with 'Chuck' and claimed 'Charlie'.

James shut the door behind him on the day's physical and professional gloom, conjuring instead his 'wine-dark sea', a full-bodied Côtes du Rhone purpling the crystal decanter in the hallway.

"Charlie? Home early, how was the fundraiser?"

No answer from any corner of their shingle-style home at Spar Cove. Charlie, an unrepentant flower child and Pasadena Art Center School of Design grad, was a local gallery owner. Her current agenda aimed at marking spring with a 'bouquet' of American Impressionism. All she lacked was a final, albeit substantial, cash injection to secure three suddenly available winners: a Benson, a Merritt Chase, and a Prendergast. She'd prepped herself accordingly that morning for a shmooze amongst Portland's wealthier denizens.

No response. No message on the hall table or the antique landline. Nobody on the property anywhere. And James, ever anxious to remain in the nineteenth century, had no cell. Maybe she'd scored a fawning zillionaire, and extra Martinis were even now sealing a cultural triumph.

James defaulted to the decanter and poured a full glass, settling into his grandmother's Quebec rocker. There were, sadly, no children to enliven the wait, but he happily thumbed the latest volume of *Antiquity*, a monthly review of archaeology. The lush photos of bronzed skin poring over fragile *objets* sifted from the Aegean never failed to warm and transport him.

At five thirty, a half-hour after the second-last ferry of the day, he'd heard nothing. James tightened up; things hadn't been perfect by any means over the last while, but there was certainly no reason to suspect some kind of 'statement' on Charlie's part.

James called several of her island intimates as well as her gallery manager on the mainland, but none had anything to report. By seven p.m., with nothing further, James seriously considered calling the Portland Police. They called first.

17

"Jamie?" He recognized the voice of Lieutenant Sanders, one of the 'classic' cops in James' thin all-star album.

"Yes, Ron…" *Why do I know, oh why!*

"Jamie, didn't want anyone coming to your door – should be me… uh, um, there's only one way to say this… about an hour ago, we got a call and, and Charlie's been found dead…"

James didn't hear himself speak. It was pure reflex.

"Where, how?"

"*The Press Hotel*, Jamie. Not accidental, we're treating it as murder – I'm so sorry Jamie."

This only happens on TV, to clients. Not me, please God!

A full two minutes passed without either speaking, the lieutenant fully indulging the personal crisis.

"I know, I know… thanks, Ron… appreciate it's difficult, appreciate you calling." *The Press?* The hotel was their favourite local escape – *but the lunch was at the College of Art. What was she…?*

"How was she…?"

"Take a moment, a deep breath, Jamie, do your best You'll want to come in – I'm sending someone. We can fill you in as far as things go then."

"*Ron.* How did Charlie die?"

No point tormenting the man. "She was apparently stabbed, multiple times. In a hallway – Jamie, take a shot, then make your way to the ferry dock; I'm sending a police launch for you."

"Right, right… okay."

"… truly sorry, she was a great gal, Jamie, and we're going to push hard, I promise."

***

Six months crawled by with no clues, no explanation, no arrest. Just a buried spouse, a beloved partner gone so incomprehensibly far before her time.

The desk clerk knew them both well, dutifully stating he'd seen Charlie enter about four thirty p.m. with an older man. Looked like they had a couple of drinks – no mystery though. Reg Weintraub was easily located, and had simply followed up on the lunch with a large cheque he didn't wish publicized. He left, and some time later, maybe five, five thirty, an 'intense' woman the clerk didn't recognize, approached Charlie, after asking if a '*Mrs.* Kirkpatrick' was there. The clerk regretted his inability to form a better description, but 'she was blonde, very white-bread you know, well-heeled and ordinary'. No such candidate had yet been fingered, and all the lunch attendees had been quickly eliminated.

The funeral was a mixed bag. A crisp, New England affair. Friends and colleagues, all supportive and disbelieving, filled the island chapel. Devastated in-laws, still ruing their daughter's being 'absconded' from the West Coast, and no parents or sister for Jamie, all having drowned years earlier in a typical Philippines ferry disaster. The wake, over in town, took the guise of a *vernissage* for the show Charlie had been curating. René, her adoring protégé from Halifax, moved robotically from piece to piece, manically expounding on brilliant details to any who would listen in an effort to avoid reality.

In June, James had the gallery sold to the art college at a cost well below market value, on condition René Savard was kept on as curator and manager, then never set foot in the place again. Having put off, and then lapsed delinquent in addressing the Pinkham complaint for months, James heaved a disgusted sigh – from pure ennui, not guilt – and quietly resigned from the bar in July. One evening in late August, he sank into the wicker chair on the front porch, glass in hand, absent his usual volume of *Antiquity*.

Instead, he cradled the new mammoth autobiography of Mark Twain; Sam Clemens knew a thing or two about personal sorrow.

In the creeping dusk, James' eye kept returning to one particular passage:

'*Twenty years from now you will be more disappointed by the things that you didn't do than by the ones you did do. So throw off the bowlines, sail away from the safe harbour. Catch the trade winds in your sails. Explore. Dream. Discover.*'

Part II

Here's to the heath, the hill and the heather,
The bonnet, the plaid, the kilt and the feather!
Tradit. Scottish toast

2

Monday, late October,
Dumfries, Scotland

Months of mourning, mental flagellation and inertia all but evaporated as James struck left off High Street. He'd dutifully 'thrown off' the bowlines, though selling *The Rigged Jury* and flying, not sailing away, to explore, discover, and hopefully dream. Promise lurked teasingly in the dark alley he now entered.

He was on the verge of admitting life might still enchant. At nine that morning, he'd stood in London Euston to catch the Brit Rail north, past the verdant hills of the Lake District, and then Carlisle, and at eight thirty that night, here he was in *Braveheart* country, sauntering into *The Globe Inn*, watering hole of Scotland's revered son, the Immortal Bard.

He'd already done a walkabout of this ancient seat of the Bruces and cultural core of the Dumfries-Galloway district, a region stretching from Gretna Green in the east along the Solway Firth and west to the Rhins of Galloway and the Irish Sea. Map names that resonated from boyhood, courtesy of Buchan, Stevenson and Sir Walter Scott.

He'd strolled over the *Auld Bridge* in the late afternoon, a link gifted in 1280 by the benevolent Lady

Devorgilla to leapfrog the marshy bogs of the River Nith, gazed down at the amber rushing over the weir and out to the Firth, and watched a mink prowling the reedy bank. From there, the centuries-old skyline rejoiced in a lack of glinting, opaque glass and canyon high-rise. Walking back to his B&B through the market square, up Shakespeare Street to Lovers' Walk, he noted the absence of any genuine rush hour, and the abundance of cobbled, pedestrian streets. Along the way, crippled and whole, poor or Harris Tweeded, all and sundry greeted him in some fashion acknowledging mutual presence on Earth.

This was a community whose core venue featured the statue of a poet, whose principal commercial and residential structure was founded in sandstone and granite.

Elegant windows and doors, old, old churches, and much greenery, infused Dumfries with an assured ambience; and of course, James joked darkly to himself as he leaned on the *Globe*'s weathered wooden bar, in *this* corner there was little chance of grim videos emerging on the Internet of orange-kilted infidels being led down Solway beaches to be decapitated. He glanced at a political flyer on the pub's noticeboard; besides, the SNP wouldn't take kindly to being upstaged.

He relished his remove from the States – his reverse 'clearance' he styled it – from Homeland paranoia, terror alerts at 'Code fuscia', pistol-packing mamas in neighbourhood Starbucks, clacking Tea Party bigots, and otherwise semi-sane citizens urging Kansas-born Muslims to 'go back where you came from'.

Yes, *Dumfries*. Or 'Dùn Phris', as the Gaelic had it, appeared this evening to open her arms to James Kirkpatrick. Though he barely knew the place, he let himself feel at home.

"And ye'll be having…?" smiled a pleasant-looking woman in perhaps her early sixties.

"Uh, let's, um, see…," which was as far as he got before the inevitable.

"Canadian?"

"No. 'Yank', you'd call me."

"Aye. Well, my aunt married one – so, ye'll be having?"

Don't let the side down James. Wait, you've left the side!

"First day here. A local ale of your choice, followed by a dram of a not too peaty Scotch. Your choice again, *please.*"

"Right then, dearie, your fate in my hands. Here we go," and the woman immediately pulled on the tap branded *Criffel*.

James leaned closer, curious, and saw below the brand name an oval depiction of blue sky, water, seabirds and cliffs: the near coast. The bottom of the frame bore the Sulwath Breweries name crowned with a thistle. The Solway Firth, had to be. *Ahhh, the real thing.* He luxuriated in the burnished fluid creaming up the pint glass. He accepted it as if Excalibur, a dripping entitlement to move among the cheerful locals, in the pub where Robbie Burns routinely inflamed his heart and liver.

The reverie of a garrulous *émigré* was pleasantly jostled by the arrival at James' elbow of a female. A willowy, veritable Pre-Raphaelite: honey-flaxen hair pulled back in a loose bun, aquiline features softened where jaw met ears, and green eyes, deeply set, with a slight droop at the outer corners lending a touch of melancholy. Tanned skin flushed by cool night air played nicely against a crisp white blouse...

The blouse also sported epaulets, a decoration bar above the left breast, and a black tie knotted from the closed collar. James refocused. He didn't need to see the navy skirt and stockings. A cop.

She was used to gawking. She let him look a second more, then half-turned.

"And you'd be from awa'?"

"Guilty," pleaded James with a sheepish though still admiring smile.

"I'm sure you are..."

Be gracious, James; this ain't the States. Not all cops yearn to hang 'em high.

"I'm thinking, not business attire. Formal occasion?"

"Funeral actually... a very sad one."

Ouch, change course.

"I'm not familiar with your insignia. You'd be a...?"

"A DCI, Detective Chief Inspector," which James very well knew from his addiction to BBC crime dramas, "if that completes your inventory?" But she seemed not at all reproving.

"My luck then, a female Morse!"

"*Re*-morse maybe," eyes brightening somewhat.

26

James persevered.

"So, they've sent the heavy artillery after me…"

The DCI perked up. A bit of banter suited the moment. Not easy burying a rookie colleague stabbed seventy-five times by a demented druggie.

"*Och*, you're deluded. You're nae a person of interest – *unless* you happen to be one, R. Burns."

"In which case…" James offered in mock apprehension.

"In which case, I'd do you for poetry under-the-influence and gross philandering."

They turned to confront each other while still propped against the bar. James saw she hadn't ordered.

"Please, no strings – and my sympathy in whatever the circumstance – can I get you a pint?"

He was new, seemed genuine, and frankly, rather bonny. Tallish, sandy hair tousled, not fussed over, and with the same hint of sadness behind light blue eyes he'd seen in hers.

"Aye," turning her head, "Jane? A Thistly Cross please."

"A…?"

"Brilliant hard cider – 'an apple a day'," wagging her finger at James.

"American, right?"

"Guilty. Not doing well, am I?" James laughed. "Does the scourge of all miscreants in the Borders have a name?"

She'd been in court and interrogation rooms too often not to recognize the enemy, Yank or no. "You'd be a barrister…"

"A criminal lawyer, once, yes – guilty yet again it seems, but now *you're* playing one."

"How so?" licking fizz very deliberately from her upper lip.

"Dodging the question."

The duly jaded, much-mentioned in dispatches DCI, teased and baited by male cronies and crooks alike, paused, then abruptly fixed on James as if administering a caution for mass child murder.

"Rodriguez."

James cocked his head slightly.

"Doesn't scream *Blue Bonnets Over the Border* does it…?" Why was she ceding all this to a perfect stranger? But, what the hell. "Took it on marriage, along with much else. My ex hated coppers, *all* coppers it turns out. Kept it though. Thought maybe championing 'social justice' under *his* name would haunt him – *ha!*" She regrouped quickly, looking up from her glass and winking at James, "Never marry a bullfighter."

"Do my best…" Must've been a grim funeral allowed James, for a senior officer to vent so. Though true, he was a safe ear as the non-local in the place. It seemed prudent not to comment.

"A first name then? Mine's James by the way, James Kirkpatrick," extending his hand. He hoped his patronym, rooted in Dumfries, would impress.

His bar-mate did a visible double take, briefly pondered something, then took his hand with a quick, warm smile. "Persephone."

28

"*Wow* – forgive me, distinctive these days, *classical.*"
He couldn't avoid his Waterhouse image now. He wanted
to spout, '*She has a lovely face; God in his mercy lend her
grace…*'

"Glad you approve. My mam liked it, she being
blessed with 'Hortense' and wishing better for her
daughter. Don't suppose you know the origin?"

This is fun, time for that Scotch. "But Miss
Moneypenny, you forget I took a first in Orientals at
Cambridge', or however it goes."

"No, *really…*"

"Of course. Daughter of Demeter and Zeus, radiant as
spring, but dwells half the year with the prince of Hades.
How's that?"

"*Shite!* I stumble round the projects and the knick, and
the only 'antiquity' I meet is the Chief Constable in his
cups, or Council hypocrisy on youth support. What'd you
read before law?"

James had routinely ducked that question from fellow
students at university; the nascent czars of mergers and
acquisitions discerned little practical value in the Periclean
light. "*Classics* with a major in archaeology.

"'*Of all the gin joints…*' Me too as it happens, at
Edinburgh. But, alas perhaps, aborted my first dig after my
father – um, was killed. Did a *volte face* and swore to dig
up scum instead of philosopher kings and queens."

"Any regrets?"

"Of course…"

Of course, indeed, James. Roads not taken. What ever
possessed *him* to advocate? Why in heaven's name had he

spurned being a khaki-shorted centerfold in *National Geo* for servitude to the criminal community? *We all stumble on the way...* he risked it all with a possible question too far.

"How'd your dad die, if you don't mind me asking?"

Persephone's face froze and she looked off. "Run down in 1999 by a drunken juvie at an SNP rally – your sort of client. Brilliant brief got him off, totally."

He'd been here before. James pressed on, ever so gently.

"Truly sorry to hear that, Persephone. Your father, I take it, was what I think you call a 'sovereigntist'?"

"Na. Ironically, but wouldnae matter I suppose. Still have his placard, stains and all: *'Don't cut it off, hold your nose and keep the union'* it read."

Best lighten things. The first twinge of a recovering libido affirmed she was indeed a buxom lass, though he was miles from baldly saying so. The mixed bonhomie of fresh arrival and premium ale, however, disgorged a compliment delivered with bowed head.

"Had my scurvy clients the privilege of being cuffed by yourself, I'd have drowned in a river of guilty pleas."

The DCI smiled at the flummery. She sensed an underlying sincerity, but didn't skip a beat.

"I doubt you're that easily defeated."

James turned to the bartender. "Jane, if I may. I need more courage, take that Scotch now – and you, Inspector?"

It was ages since she'd let her hair down, at the shop or anywhere else. She was sloughing off a mournful day, and a tipple more could hasten her path to a peaceful bed.

"Why not then? Ta..."

Jane made a fine show of retrieving a secreted bottle and filling two antique dram glasses. *"Càrn Mòr.* Speyside, aged fifteen years in the cask, only 400 bottles produced," she confided, happy to see her favourite constable pleasantly engaged.

"To great cops and great lawyers, *all two of us!"* declared James, as the forensic veterans clinked and sipped in brief silence.

"And to Justice, *wherever* she hides," added Persephone.

"Right on," James muttered, loathe to touch that one. "Wow!" he whistled after a second sip. "Wish I was an aficionado and could comment impressively, but I know enough to sense a classy nectar. Should really do an in-depth study of single malts."

"A nobler calling I'm sure, counsel," Persephone shot back, setting her glass on the counter. "But *my* sheets are calling, and I must awa'." She looked him squarely in the eye, as if a respected equal. "For a brief, and a male, you're aye a good listener. Thanks for the crack and restorative beverages."

"Safe home, Persephone Rodriguez, and thank *you*," and they shook hands.

The damp air and her stress-stained uniform heightened anticipation of warm covers, so it wasn't till she was out the inn door that the vaunted mistress of interrogation realized she hadn't asked the fella his purpose in town. As for James, he found himself flushed and staring at the siren sway of the departing officer. Rarely had he felt so drawn to the long arm.

31

A final dram seemed entirely appropriate. Jane winked approvingly as she poured it. He drew on it slowly, savouring his new 'situation', whatever that might be, while casually scanning a detailed tourist map of Dumfries and Galloway he'd picked up during the day.

A veteran 'salt', James instinctively searched for islands running off the west coast. Trailing down the Sea of the Hebrides were the three 'small Isles': Rum, the one sitting below it, Eigg, and then the lesser, third isle farther below, Nog, surely – but *no*, it was Muck! James laughed out loud. *Guess it depends on how you mix them.*

His eye moved down to the mouth of the Solway Firth at Cairnryan and the Irish Sea. A tiny, solitary dot sat a few kilometres offshore, rejoicing in the name, Ailsa Craig. *Wild*, thought James. Like some ancient 'hag' from a children's tale; '*sleep tight, or Ailsa will rattle your window!*'

James folded the map, patted down a hefty tip, shook Jane's hand because he damn well felt like it, then more or less floated up English Street. Serendipity alone deposited him eventually at *The Clog and Thistle,* where, after a mere five attempts, he succeeded in fitting the key in the front door.

He drifted off beneath a glorious duvet, the word 'Galloway' running over and over through his mind. Like a night-steed, stretching and snorting fiercely, galloping, galloping for the coast...

3

8:30 a.m., Tuesday
Dumfries town centre

The sun sparkling off the River Nith beckoned. The day was unusually warm for autumn in the Lowlands. Back in Maine they'd call it an Indian summer. James poured his java, 'American coffee', into a take-away cup and exited *Scrumptious*, the cozy vault in Rugman's Hall, a seventeenth century merchant's house, to cross to the riverbank. Once on the promenade, the moment drew James 200 metres even further, back to the *Auld Bridge* for the second time in twenty-four hours. Deeming himself a resident now, he decided to luxuriate in pondering the ducks flapping ludicrously up the weir, the stream beneath, and life generally.

He ambled up the eastern steps onto the arched span, only to find another person similarly inspired, a woman, leaning over the stone parapet in the middle. She wore an oatmeal turtleneck, fitted dark leather jacket, and short grey skirt. No navy stockings. James didn't hesitate to share his loner's pursuit.

"Don't do it, Officer – so much to live for!"

Persephone Rodriguez smiled slowly without looking up. "Naa, naa. Just reflecting…"

"Often happens when leaning over water."

Pause. Persephone straightened up and winced demonstrably. "*Very* clever, counsel. I see the authorities have not yet deported you. My fault, I never asked why ye're with us. And for the record, it's a tad shallow for hurling oneself in from here, though a lad has floated up with the melting ice from time to time."

James seized the opportunity.

"All right, I'll confess, on condition you still consider me a 'person of interest'. I'm here tracing genealogy; surprise, surprise. But also – promise not to cringe – using whatever I turn up to attempt a book. A 'crime' novel actually. No threat to Rendall or Rankin for sure, more of a *'why'd*-they-do-it' than a *'who*-dunnit'…"

"And what drove you to sic drastic state of affairs?"

James wasn't emotionally ready to recount specifics. There was candour, though, in relating how, 'recently', he'd been shaken when re-reading one of his early, obscure icons, Gerald Brenan. The decorated WWI veteran and British expat, fringe member of Bloomsbury, had decamped to Andalusia, where, in describing the rigidity of Spanish peasant culture, he noted how those with dreams had withered by age thirty, and how, by forty, 'looked like a pressed fern in an album'.

"I'd been thinking, what's my life-to-date worth if I don't make an effort to strain it with some kind of new direction, some introspection or literary analysis, the end product ideally masked in a gripping tale of human foibles?"

The DCI, amused, nevertheless listened intently. "Sounds like ye've at least got the jacket blurb well in hand."

In for a penny, in for a pound. James continued.

"Happens the Dumfries region is our family seat, and a 'return' always lurked on the old bucket list, and, well, there's much I've left behind – or maybe, not much at all – anyway, my grandfather was a second generation Kirkpatrick from Nova Scotia, married a Flanagan he met from around here during the Second World War. My idea was to inject local lore into – I don't know – a cold case of some sort. Fashion quaint facts into fiction…"

The copper couldn't resist.

"Hmm, exactly what you did all those years for juries. Should be easy."

"*Touché*. But, maybe *you* could vet some of my scenarios in due course," and James looked over the parapet. "Should check for sodden bodies sailing by…"

"I could arrange a romantic visit to the morgue, stare the real thing in the face."

"Thanks, I'm sure, but mirrors already do that for me!" Then the prior evening kicked in. "We *could* do better. Unless I get lucky with an underage schoolgirl, or a rich, terminally ill widow, I've no one to share gruel with tonight, or *any* night for that matter – *you* must have a favourite bistro. Be my guest and share it?"

Twice met on grim days at the office, fair repartee, and nice legs actually. Persephone was inclined. It had been bludy ages…

"I've a rotten media briefing at end-of-day, then assorted dolts and duty call, but keep me on your Pulitzer invite list till Friday, if you can. Meet you at *Little Italy* at eight thirty. Bonny *scran*, run by a genial Serb of all things."

"Done!" The rest of his day shone even brighter. "Onlookers will be expecting me to hand you a plain brown envelope, so I best withdraw," and James waved, and all but skipped off the bridge as if he'd scored for the Prom.

***

To my inheritance amid the nation that is not…
A. E. Housman

The 'rest of his day', and indeed the week, was consumed in diligent, sometimes awestruck musing amongst the stones and ghosts of generations.

The wandering hours were mossy and 'old world', profoundly resonant of childhood books and James' lifelong romance with history. When he wasn't scouring the tales below grass, he found himself often, after an early tip from a passing stranger, simply drifting on the Long Walk by the river, further shedding personal loss and scabrous court battles like petals. James 'listened', in the mornings and afternoons, to thundering hooves, bells peeling in village spires, the roar of cannon, and the collective wail of monarchs, mothers, wives, lovers and inevitably, the blessed pipes.

Following the bridge encounter with Persephone, his initial sortie had taken him a mere block up from the river. There at the corner of Broom's Road and St Michael's Street, he confronted a hillock anchoring St Michael's, a church with a thousand years of history. Huge sandstone or marble tablets slanted at all angles from the ancient turf, in some stretches forming a wall, honeycombing all sides of the house of worship of Robbie Burns and his faithful wife, Jeanne Armour, through the waning years of the eighteenth century.

Within the first minutes, a truism leapt out at James: cemeteries hold all the plot (*poor pun, James*) fodder a budding scribe could wish for. Archaic names and occupations, wrenching swathes of infant mortality, plague, fever and persecution, the 'perished at sea' migrants and far-flung King's sailors. He revelled in his singular quest, gravitating wherever archives, church registers, graveyards and wonderfully discursive locals urged.

Throughout that week, of all the region's cemeteries, war and other memorials – including the profound tributes in nearby Lockerbie – kirks, municipal scrolls and records, distinctive architecture like *Robert the Bruce*, a cavernous, magnificently windowed pub in a grand structure on Buccleuch Street, it was hoary old St Michael's which first and foremost held the match to James' imagination. It was there he had the first glimpses of his own lineage; there too, eclectic threads and potential themes were whispered to him by the not-so-silent tenants.

Even as James found the front door of St Michael's locked that morning, and was poking round the west side for the vestry, he came on a specimen of stoic *brevitas* etched into the brick wall:

Here lies
William Veitch
1640-1722
Covenanter, persecuted and banished
Suffered but survived
Minister of the Parish 1694-1715
also
His praying, supportive wife, Marion
who predeceased him by one day

"Eighty-two, aye. Survived a braw stretch."

Observing James from the vestry door was the prototypical, benign cleric, a dead ringer from a BBC period drama.

"Hmm," managed James.

"Indeed, sir, three wars and 'the killing time' – we *are* closing for the moment, but you're aye a visitor. From?"

"The States, but I intend to stay. Family roots here…"

"Welcome, w*elcome!* Come in then," he said, fluttering a pale, graceful hand. "Thomas McClounie, the verger. Have been forty-five years, an' dootless look it."

"James Kirkpatrick," as they shook hands and proceeded through the sacristy into the chancel.

"Kirkpatrick? Then ye're safe hame, laddie! Lots o' *them* aboot, thick as thieves wi' the Bruce, ye ken?"

His first peek about engaged James immediately. Predominant smooth aged stone, warm wooden pews, a spiralling wooden staircase off the entrance to the choir, and a wooden screen masking the entrance, inset with a matching pair of stain glass portraits of Robert Burns and Jeanne Armour.

"Aye then, I'm nae quick on my feet, but if ye've the time, I'll gie the grand tour! Have a seat, there, beside that pillar, aye. That's Robbie's pew. His wife Jean sat there every Sunday for thirty years after his death. He was nae mad wi' it like people clype. Leapt into the Solway with his sword in 1792 to help capture a smugglers' brig. The Royal Dumfries Volunteers lined the streets at his funeral and the Angusshire Fencibles fired three volleys over his grave. Just outside there, in the far corner ye ken, before they moved him to the mausoleum..."

James was genuinely enthralled by this special guide, and soon felt like a tippling, romantic laureate, but a chilly frisson shot down his neck when the good verger at length moved into 'the battles of the '45'.

"*Charlie* was here of course...", jolting James upright. "*Ach*, I see your interest there – aye, he was in Dumfries rallying Jacobites during one of his retreats. Demanded £2000 and a thousand pairs o' clogs. *Weel*, the town surrendered only £1195 and 225 pairs o' clogs. He laid brush against the walls of the church and set fire to it. Nae muckle luved for that!"

Fifteen brogue-numbed minutes later, McClounie parked his Epistle to the Jamesians to lead the willing pilgrim outside and down the eastern path to Burns' death-white mausoleum. There he left James to his musings, which were by then swirling with the realization he now paced the ground of his fathers. Gazing back over the huge monographs of drapers, cabinet makers, soldiers and merchant mariners, to the square-towered church spire, he began to imagine unfolding melodramas. Bonneted women, claymore-brandishing rogues, buxom whisky servers, and most clearly, lads staring down the Nith, dreaming of distant shores: long dormant, yet vibrant tales hovering in the fresh Solway air!

James lingered, happily scribbling down names, dates, wild scenarios of crime, lust and greed for nearly two hours, until a noon pint strongly suggested itself, and he made his way out of the kirkyard, pausing to thank the verger, by then re-stationed at his desk inside the vestry.

"Aye, ye're most welcome, sir. Please *do* come to the harvest celebration next Sunday…"

"Thank you very much, Thomas. See if I can gather a sheaf or two."

"*Och!* I'm thinking best not leave afore ye look on the east wall o' the chancel, through there again. Aye, the large plaque…"

The interloper from Maine scanned as directed: … *in loving remembrance of the men of this congregation who laid down their lives for their country in the Great War.* His eye moving steadily till it rested on the name topping the second column:

Kirkpatrick, James

40

Crossing St Michael's Street the short distance to the *Ship Inn*, James shook his head slowly after viewing the Kirkpatrick link climaxing his little tour; he felt light on his feet, as if invisibly conveyed. If he weren't meant to be there, the memorial blast from Flanders certainly defied reason: who said history didn't vibrate at your toes? *Imagine*, James admonished himself, *here I am plunked in this old pub, in the town where my ancestors lived, loved, fought and died, and in due course, were laid in the sod just steps away.*

As his daily 'whisky lesson', a fifteen-year-old Islay single malt, Bruichladdich, was set down, James reached for a copy of *The Herald* from a wall rack. The news from Dumfries was not nearly as sunny as his explorer's disposition. The front page featured a colour photo of a blood-soaked venue down a town lane. Grisly, and as he read it, a vague relevance percolated.

The young male victim was apparently an 'advanced highers' student boarding locally, an escapee from a turbulent estate in Lanarkshire called Goŵkthrapple.

Conditioned to impose levity on horror, James instantly scoffed, the name might well constitute an offence of itself: '*James Kirkpatrick, you are charged with murder, in that you did, with malice aforethought, strangle one, Robert Hapless, by means of a Goŵkthrapple...*

The murder, a slash and stab affair, had actually been achieved by means of an ancient claymore and an 'early Scottish dirk', the latter further described by the intrepid reporter as a 'direct descendant of the mediaeval bullock dagger'. That much was known of the MO, as the

41

weapons, commendably, had been recovered from the reeds of the Nith, which flowed past White Sands, the river street at the bottom of the lane in question. No motive had yet been determined. *Gruesome*, winced James, but as levity again surfaced, certainly a crime with an element of pageantry. Perhaps some history buffs got carried away.

'Buffs' in the plural, as providentially, the single night's immersion in brackish water had apparently not erased two distinct sets of different palm and fingerprints, one discrete set on each weapon. A long-ago police seminar James attended resurfaced: water didn't necessarily erase latent prints if the objects in question were smooth-surfaced, carefully dried and the hands in question had been sweaty or greasy.

Authorities were thus seeking *two* perps. Seemed odd to James that two were required to dispatch one, a teen at that. To his knowledge, 'swarming' hadn't become endemic in the UK.

Maybe something to engage Persephone with while sampling vintages that Saturday…

4

Moffat Road, Dumfries

"Amazing. Couldn't have scripted this if I tried..."

James looked around, arms raised expansively, as he and Persephone were seated in the upstairs gallery by the amiable owner of *Little Italy*, an attractive stone resto just a pleasant stroll over a small bridge from the B&B, and up a lushly residential street.

"I mean, Scottish locale, Serbian host, Mediterranean menu, a riveting, classically educated minion of HM's constabulary, and a handsome American ambulance chaser, collaborating over fine Chianti, whisky to follow!"

Persephone rolled her eyes in droll horror. James barely noticed, confronted as he was by a lilac spaghetti strap that did admirable justice to the law.

"'Collaborating'?"

"At your service, Inspector. And why not? With our combined store of brilliant insight, there must be a cold case, a Holmes-baffler, we can tackle together. No fee asked; throw me the facts, see how we do!"

Persephone was, frankly, already curious to see how they 'did', but not in the pursuit of law and order.

"Gotta *luv* amateurs, James, lad. Get thee to Glasgow, the *Scottish Centre for Crime and Justice Research*. Troll through the gory data; it'll better serve your tome-to-be, and tonight… tonight, why don't we ramble instead through ancient Greece and the glories of Dionysian excess?"

"Not even that local teen's murder I read about in the *Herald*?"

"*Especially* not that. A right *oovas*!"

"I humbly accept your terms, Persephone…"

"'Seph', if ye'll be a decent fella, despite being a lawyer…"

"'Seph' it is! All right then, into the Castalian springs, shall we? Bring on the vino!"

The keen eavesdropper would next have been intrigued by the couple's avid cavorting below Parnassus, as if they'd emerged only moments earlier from the lecture hall. At least two hours sailed by, exchanging eccentric 'prof' anecdotes, favourite Catullan odes, architectural splendours, and following – or more accurately, in the wake of – a 1966 Meursault, the drowsy potpourri of a Pommard, and a mutual vow to pursue a diving adventure in the Gulf of Argos. James' head swam with visions of golden skin, souvlaki, and whitewashed stones leading down to the royal blue…

In midst of reverie, Persephone retrieved her inquisitor's bent. "But James, since we're tripping in the silt of eons: I told you how *my* 'roads taken' happened. What's *your* alibi for dropping the golden bough?"

His brow furrowed. He'd never really analyzed it all these years, never discussed his decision with anyone, or felt the need to, even with Charlie, but he tried now. James was increasingly at ease in telling this copper anything she wished to hear.

"My friends used to mock me. 'What're you gonna do with a Classics degree? Teach Latin like some pathetic Mr Chips in a mangy prep school in Vermont?' I got to laugh a bit in my graduating summer, when my swimmer's background landed me a Ford Foundation grant and a spot as a diver on a dig off the coast of Marathon. Died and gone to heaven. Hardly wore clothes, sun and ocean, history lurking under every stone. Fresh fish dinners, cold *Hellas* beer, *karpouzi* for dessert under a canopy by the sea at nine p.m. Where did I go wrong…?"

Persephone's green eyes moistened at seeing the deeper ponds she'd rather hoped to see.

"… and then, what was I going to do for a living while I tried to forge a *lifelong* 'dig'? I rationalized, or maybe duped myself, that a *true* 'English' education – I'd always respected that notion because so many classical scholars were English – comprised reading Classics, then reading law. The complete man if you will. So I got myself into Rutgers and then when my second degree rolled in, had to confront the 'making a living' bit again. Having been a loner to a certain extent in courting the ancient world, it was natural I guess to be a defence attorney; you know, the Lone Ranger riding into town to stick up for the little guy… and those, for better or worse, are the sad facts of my case, your delightful Honour." He felt oddly refreshed, unburdened.

Persephone was hungry, but not yet ready to be ravenous. She lolled in a full-mouth, long and delicious

45

kiss when their evening met the street outside, and there was little doubt both professional and emotional instinct were on track. The suspect hardly stood a chance.

***

James was once again exiting *Scrumptious*, his adopted morning launch pad, floating on the aftertaste of real blackcurrant jam and thick, fluffy scones, when a squad car roared up beside him, blue light flashing, and the driver leapt out to block his way.

"*You*, sir!"

"Madam!"

"Aye Mr Kirkpatrick, caught in broad daylight. Hearken to me. Been mindful of last night and you swanning about the premises, haunting the kirkyards, draining our best whisky. Thought you could do something *useful* for our juvenile folk."

A startled grin spread over the apprehended's face. Novel fun, flirting with the law.

"But, Inspector, I gave at the office – *whoops !* No, I abandoned the office. Better give me details, make your pitch."

"Put you back in school, rejuvenate your battered psyche. There's a programme..." The weathered male colleague in the passenger's seat looked bewildered at his guv, chatting so amicably with a total stranger. "Personal whim really, sold the Council coots on it. Many of these hoodies lack any compass, let alone hope for their world; they flaunt an ignorance and disdain of the law. I do my

46

best – when *behold*, along comes yersel, bursting with the glory of the process, redemption, human victories in court…"

Persephone's eyes danced wickedly. "You *had* some, din't ye!"

James was shamelessly flattered. The surprise overture was invigorating, both for pen and ego. His summer's earlier epiphany replayed. Sorting things after Charlie's death, he'd scanned his study shelf and pulled down a favourite. The jacket photo showed David Cornwell striding along Cornish sea cliffs, plotting the next twist of human frailty, before – word had it – repairing to the local for a single malt, or three. James had thereafter modelled his literary idyll in Scotland to emulate the lean spy, religiously. But he saw his 'arrest' at the hands of the lovely Persephone as no impediment; rather, a siren call to be heeded, and certainly a legit source of creative gist.

"What d'ye say? Evil defence counsel, full of sad tales of spotty youth shagged by the system. You can enlighten the wee buggers. No fee ken, payment only in improving pub sessions."

"Fair enough, Officer. And of course, they won't be distracted by *my* legs."

"Lippy bastard! So, we're on then. I'll hold the cuffs, this time. Start tomorrow. Pick you up right here, one sharp, just a jog over to the Academy." Persephone jumped back into the squad car and leaned out the window, smiling sweetly. "Really, James, you'll love it, raging hormones. Bring lots of Clearasil."

The police fled the scene leaving two elderly women shoppers baffled but well armed for their coffee chat. James crossed the street, then over the Nith on an elegant nineteenth-century suspension bridge to set up office on a park bench. Pad and pencil in hand, he anticipated genuine pleasure in obliging the cause of local teens, i.e DCI Rodriguez.

Minutes later, it came as joint revelation and intellectual luxury to sit under russet branches by a foreign river, sifting through 'a life in court'. James was amazed at how long and inhabited his actual hallway of cautionary tales was.

5

Monday
1:15 p.m.

Dumfries Academy, founded in 1804, is set back on a slight elevation from, appropriately, Academy Street. Its massive sandstone façade is well riddled with tall windows, and the entrance lies through a central Ionic portico. Very rampant lions guard the corners of the roof cupola, crowned by a gilt lady bearing aloft the beacon of learning. A plaque at the front steps proclaims that exalted alumni include *Sir James M. Barrie, 1860-1937*, progenitor of *Peter Pan*.

Today, the current generation streamed around two older visitors, wreathed in cheap scents, raw body odour, and slathered locks glistening in the sun. The immediate crowd cascaded in chatter and goggle-eyed animation, when not glued to various devices. James felt instantly decrepit.

"Shocker, in't, lad?"

"Seems I left my walker at home," mumbled James. The American myth of the individual didn't spoil his pleasure at the kineticism animating figures and faces in school uniform. White shirts, wine and silver-striped ties, loose-knotted of course, dark blazers and sweaters, grey pants, or skirts, hiked up, lent an air of common purpose

49

starkly contrasting with the metal detectors and resident police back in the 'good old'.

James and Persephone passed into the hallowed halls, and were met at the door of Room 105 by a young female teacher who keyed immediately on James.

"Faith Richardson, *History, Heritage and Society*," she said, vigorously shaking James' hand. "The inspector assures me you're a renowned advocate and inspiring speaker."

"Indeed," scowling at his partner. "Remind me to waterboard her later."

Into the valley…

The classroom was suppressed mayhem, but strangely familiar. Hair dominated the confronting throng: braided, shaved, Mohawked, greased. Shiny faces, rings in odd places and a pervasive babble which, to be honest, James found infectious. Such jangling vitality, such innocent will not yet in collision with an unforgiving world.

Persephone wrapped up a quick intro, in which she hyped James as a veritable Clarence Darrow and connoisseur of sensational depravity. Males in the back row listened all agog for all the wrong reasons. "Well, ye've all heard me blether about why you should shun the nick, a drug record, worship your health, keep free of a bad past as you start out; but here's Mr Kirkpatrick, all across from America, to 'tell it like it is' as they say over there. His name alone should make him welcome in Dumfries."

James absorbed the inspector's wink and walked to the small lectern on the teacher's desk. A glance over the room, obviously well stacked for the occasion, killed any notion of a turgid discourse on the glorious, organic nature of the rule of law. The female students appeared mainly women on the verge, the males, nearly shorn of gawkiness. In instant sum, the class exuded a dynamic though unfocused intellect, a minor explosion not yet triggered.

He chose to lead with the tale of a rural murder in Maine: the farmer with the antique scythe, the Swiss *au pair* in the barnyard tub, and how a nearby tethered horse emerged as the key witness. To illustrate the principle of deterrence, he followed with the callous American nightmare of death row and its illusory deterrence.

"Sir, what's it like to be on a jury?"

"Lawyers aren't allowed to serve on them, but maybe *you'll* get the experience. More educational than a thousand spiels like mine!" But the query opened the way for several trial anecdotes on the sometimes humorous, often quirky psychology of juries. By then, James felt midway in his guest slot and the audience's charity, and thought a bit of 'guidance' appropriate and expected. He extolled their youth, the world was definitely theirs to question, but the way could be made much smoother by acknowledging some realities.

"In case you hadn't noticed, outside home and school, life can be a jungle; it's sometimes healthier to take the beaten path and not get strangled by the vines. What do I mean? I mean, for example – and don't zoom me by saying, like our former President, most of you haven't 'inhaled' (amazingly, some knowing sniggers) – save your money and time for travel, give drugs and material fads the finger. A zombie majority of Americans stagger around daily on over-prescription or street products, and it's subverted our entire society, distorted our justice system, bankrupted state correction authorities, fed racism, even poisoned international relations – think Mexico, Colombia – and debased our national integrity. That sweeping enough?"

This unleashed a torrent of questions generally proposing the pragmatic decision to legalize *all* drugs, thus deterring organized crime and guaranteeing quality through regulation. James dodged the bullet by applauding their wisdom 'ahead of the curve', but such a regime was politically distant in its eventuality, and teasingly, was their interest possibly in still being able to 'enjoy' the debilitating distraction? In the immediate term, better to exalt their bodies and personal health.

"Every toke or snort paid for here in your beautiful Lowlands allows some scum elsewhere to laugh all the way to the bank. In short, don't be an *eejit* – forgive that; I love your slang. Please understand, 85% of all meth, coke, hash, ecstasy, you name it, is not what they say it is. How in hell you think they make a fortune? Selling pure stuff at a discount? While you writhe in agony after a warehouse rave, dealers chuckle in the sun in Mallorca. Listen, here's a dose of annoying reality on the bottom line: after the privilege of chatting with you, I'm probably going to enjoy a single malt at the pub; and you may very well say alcohol's just another drug, so where do *I* get off spouting warnings. But here's the thing, *life's not fair*, and it's plain reality that downing that dram won't cause my arrest, a job-crippling record, or a tainted or fatal overdose… You're all *so lucky*, well on your way, getting a great education, smart enough to respect the law without feeling smothered by it or being mocked by others less cool. *Rejoice* in keeping on track!"

No cheers at this juncture, but some encouraging frowns of reflection. Persephone nodded gently, pleased with her catch for the programme; Faith Richardson positively glowed with this authentic, yet not self-absorbed speaker. She even wondered which 'pub' he had in mind.

"Well, no more cheap wisdom folks, except this little corollary to what I was just running on about: *true* freedom is not unqualified; *chaos* is the direct default of everyone 'doing their own thing' with no regard for social harmony or others. The law is an invisible *shield* against an often vicious world, not a handcuff…"

He could see a few hands straying to their devices: time to make *their* world relevant.

"All right then, speaking of chaos, what of the world-wide web? Instant, viral exposure for oceans of bigoted, ill-informed or malicious crap. The banality of evil, boring and destructive, and yet, arguably, the so-called 'last bastion' of free speech ? Should it remain the ungated launch pad for morons, jihadists or pedophiles?"

That paused the texting; but James suspected it was like asking drunks if they considered booze problematic. A few brave souls praised the Web as aiding a more cohesive global society, spurring initiative, eliminating the drudgery from research; but most prattled on about how it instantly linked friends and associates. How vital it was to stay 'connected'.

James lightened up with a wildly eclectic 'all-time fave' list of films with a legal motif. "Get some popcorn or crisps and enjoy these movies as pure entertainment, but, they also illustrate what tough choices and integrity can achieve, Twitter and Instagram notwithstanding…" The list: "*Twelve Angry Men, The Verdict, Witness for the Prosecution, The Winslow Boy, A Few Good Men, Inherit the Wind, To Kill a Mockingbird,* and I could go on," which Ms Richardson also realized.

"Perhaps, Mr Kirkpatrick, as Inspector Rodriguez tells me you have long-term intentions in Dumfries, you could host a 'courtroom film festival' some time in the future, as a companion to the course," and she smiled genuinely.

"Would be a pleasure, ma'am." Time to wrap up.

"Let me leave you with this: the law's a comforter, not a wet blanket. You may read occasionally of police abuse, shocking miscarriages of justice, etc., but generally, you live in a privileged country where people like Inspector Rodriguez put themselves in harm's way day after day, dealing with slobbering drunks, vomiting druggies, violent thugs and endless sneers and prejudice. And yet, she finds time to come here and encourage you, with real-life experience, to be the best you can be."

There was a spontaneous burst of applause, and Persephone blushed deeply despite herself.

"We'll have two more questions only, everyone…"

A very shy, intense-looking girl, stood up ramrod straight, but looking to one side, and asked haltingly, as if to the world in general, "Do you... think they'll catch whoever killed Alan?"

"Alan?"

A sudden pall befell the room.

"Ahh... Alan Sanderson, our poor classmate found in the side street last week," Richardson quietly interposed.

"Oh yes, *yes*, read about it in the paper. I know such tragedy is hard to absorb, especially when the victim is a friend, and so very young. A bit of a mystery as I understand it; but, I should think your question is really one more for the inspector."

"We're exhausting absolutely every effort, Abith," Persephone volunteered, with her encyclopedic memory for names.

"Well, then... what I really mean to ask, is, should there be – if they capture them, er, him, or her – will there be a harsher sentence for killing a young person?" And she sat down, or rather shrank back into her seat, but then immediately popped up again.

"... and, and on the other hand, if it's a young person too, the killer, should they be treated more leniently, or...?"

This time, Abith sat down more emphatically, glancing nervously, however, to her right, apologizing perhaps for her awkwardness.

James wanted to respect the question.

"Well, it depends on the particular jurisdiction. Some have specified limits on juvenile penalties, and it may vary with the crime or the aggravated nature of its commission. As far as the victim's age, that could itself be an aggravating determinant. For the record, and call me a Pollyanna, I tend to favour a second bite of the apple for young offenders. In my experience, invariably, no matter how tough the sentence, family and friends are never satisfied or at peace with it, and 'closure' is empty jargon. At the same time, however, no matter how desolate the personal landscape of the perpetrator, for those in a happier, more privileged position to simply throw away the key seems too easy, a denial of life's potential."

"Final question," chirped the teacher.

A momentary silence, before the spindly arm of the lad seated to the prior questioner's right snaked upwards.

"Yes?"

"Sir, you said," in a reedy, high-pitched voice, "the world's not always fair. So, justice won't always happen, on either side of the violent interaction, right?"

James thought that rather an elevated phrasing of the issue. "I can hear thunderous applause for that sad fact from O. J. Simpson, or a bevy of ex-Nazi death camp commandants."

"So, we're supposed to let evil persons go free even if we know who he is, and the law, or society, may never deal with them?"

Where's this going? wondered James, though certainly intrigued.

"Are you asking if we should take matters into our own hands at a certain point, possibly even where the issue hasn't become technically criminal? Bearing in mind our

56

despicable American experience with lynch mobs and vigilantism..."

The young provocateur looked like he was slipping in and out of a trance before he suddenly shot back, "Yes. Otherwise, what's it worth being victimized, or, or, to know you're right, if nothing's done, if *you* don't take some control..."

"Purely speculating then, it might depend on exactly what it is you 'do'– you're not talking about taking a life, I trust?"

The student turned vague again. "It, well, you have to make sure the wrong, the evil, doesn't continue."

Perhaps time for a segue, thought James.

"Well, there's not an easy all-purpose answer, but, thank you for a tough question, and whatever you *should* do, I recommend keeping the inspector's card handy!"

Some laughter, and the questioner was left staring resolutely out the window for a second or two before folding back into his seat.

"Thank you, Mr Kirkpatrick. For a fresh, *streetwise* insight on criminal law. Please come back anytime! Right, everyone?"

A healthy round of applause and some whistles. The room emptied and Richardson led her two guests out the Academy portal.

"That really was a treat, Mr Kirkpatrick..."

"James, please."

"James. You handled that last lad well if I may say so. To be frank, he's something of an enigma. History is his obsession. In fact, he's won a Cambridge entrance scholarship – but a painful-seeming loner. Gay, I'm pretty certain – which is entirely irrelevant to be sure – but effeminate mannerisms and that voice have, I fear, inspired serious bullying or abuse of some sort."

Persephone invoked 'the street' on behalf of her guest. "Life's not fair, as James said. Maybe Cambridge will bleach the stigma."

They all shook hands, James promising to return another time, and the two 'legals' made a beeline for *The Globe Inn*.

The unsinkable Jane Brown greeted them effusively.

"*Ach*, the law still mixing with the law. Smacks o' incest!"

James went for a *Criffel*, by now his 'usual', and Persephone, a G&T, thinking to prep herself for the next week's professional schedule.

"So then, James, I'm off to Edinburgh for a refresher on weapons and emergency response. Be back the weekend. You'll nae miss me I'm sure, with your various exhumations and all those drams to flush the writer's block…"

"Ha! You can proof any drafts, after I scrape off the moss and dirt."

The inspector sucked voraciously on her lime.

"By the way, hearing that young victim's name, 'Alan Sanderson', reminds me. Any breaks in that affair, the 'Bad-apple' case?"

"*Goŵkthrapple* you cretin. Naa, just, whoever they were, they weren't pros. Too many shallow wounds; coroner suggests it might be ritualistic, hinting maybe at

58

older types." She looked over her shoulder fetchingly. "Old-fashioned picnic at the sea if you solve it for us mere locals while I'm awa'."

For the second time in James' presence, Persephone unbundled her honey tresses, prompting him to scratch a hasty IOU for a seaside picnic on a bar napkin and hand it over for her signature.

"So, what'd ye think, the Academy and all?"

"Whew! Took me back, Seph. All those kinetic, distracted faces, all that promise… but thanks, *truly*. Hope I helped the cause. Must admit though, glad not to be suffering through that phase again. Quite content to be where I am right now."

"Me too," said she, blindsided by her romantic doubletake on James' admission.

6

There's nothing to writing. All you do is sit down... and open a vein.
Red Smith

Old jeans, penny loafers without socks, a well-worn navy turtleneck: James felt comfortably old-hat in his new environs. No whining clients, no court, no drones descending from the Bar Association. No banal logistics of house and boat maintenance, though he genuinely missed the latter manual therapy, and vowed to launch himself on the Solway Firth sooner rather than later.

And then of course, tragically enough, there was no 'other' in his life to look out, or wait for. Even Seph, his new – friend, colleague, Gaelic muse? – was engaged elsewhere that week, so his creative juice could flow at will.

But there was no 'starving artist in the garret' in James' current scenario. The expat luxuriated in second coffees on the stone patio at the back of the *Clog and Thistle* in the morning sun, closing his eyes to conjure scenes to enthral and ambush readers. When the spirit moved – and it did frequently – he 'perambulated' (a favourite word he struggled to keep out of his writing) about the old kirkyards, digging up more names and inspiration. And whenever rain encouraged, he ransacked the archives of Dumfries and Galloway on Catherine Street, congratulating himself on tracking the inked history of local humanity.

Sandy Tweedsmuir, the thirty-something archivist, was receptive to this foreign researcher. James' rookie enthusiasm soon led her to dubbing him the 'Yankee raider'. She delighted in steering him through the region's eighteenth-century 'Police Criminal Album', 'Jail Books', 'Council Minutes', 'Kirk Sessions', and 'Shipping Register'.

By the week's end, James had come face to signature with *Robt. Burns, Excise Officer*, several times, and now felt stowed with enough Lowland lore to sink a coastal smuggler. On Thursday, it teemed with rain as if God missed the Flood, so James politely dodged the landlady's sandwiches, aiming to pursue a lunch tip from Persephone.

The tip was *Pumpernickel*, a café embedded in an alley running off the central square that boasted Greyfriars' Kirk and the famous marble statue of Burns. The alley ran straight down to the Nith. The DCI had urged the grilled cheese and *any* of the soups, 'lovingly homemade, good for an all-American laddie'.

James ordered and ate as directed. The deluge outside fed his comfort inside. It was utter contentment to mix savoury mouthfuls with shrewd, though undisciplined, editing of his virgin drafts.

Thus far, his novice pen flirted with death and desire, and how they had ravaged a Highland family in the early 1800s. More than a generation after Culloden, sons and fathers battled claims of treachery during the Young

Pretender's cause, railed against eviction, and cursed the absentee lairds and their ubiquitous sheep. The family's upheaval would in due course transit to Solway shores and an agonizing struggle between just enduring, and far horizons: Canada and America called. Ships would sail 'awa''. Wives and daughters of course, would bear their superior wisdom in silence, it being the nineteenth century, and they would die in droves from childbirth, consumption or plain disgust A salt-laced murder on embarkation would resonate into the twenty-first century, but James had still to contrive the shocking nexus.

No title had yet firmly sold itself. *Clandestiny* was one, but far too cute; *Blood in the Heather* another, but for the moment, *A Skirl of Malice* held sway as working banner.

Tickled by his cleverness, James nearly missed two figures passing outside his window table. Teenagers, one female, the other, hooded, most probably male. For an instant, the girl's drenched hair parted as she looked furtively around, allowing James to discern one of the questioners from his Academy visit. He actually stood from his table to better observe, as it was surprising to recognize anybody so soon in his new domicile.

Despite the downpour, the pair stopped a few metres further along and proceeded to scrutinize, mysteriously, the wall on the side opposite the café. They remained on the spot for several minutes, shifting back and forth, then suddenly disappeared down the way. Whatever held their eye was obscured from James; pure curiosity determined him to see for himself when the skies abated.

The heavens smiled thirty minutes later and James paid his tab, joking with the manager that he intended to make the place famous with a reference in his forthcoming bestseller. He exited *Pumpernickel*, turning immediately left to reach the spot earlier occupied by the two transients. As best he could make out, the obvious focus of their attention had to have been a large mural panel, roughly seven feet by twelve feet and framed in sandstone; the small building on whose wall it was set looked long vacant. A scroll atop the mural read:

'Friars Vennel', once the site of
Greyfriars Monastry where in 1306
Robert the Bruce
Slew the Red Comyn aided by Sir Roger
Kirkpatrick and opened the final stage for
Scottish independence which ended
victoriously at Bannockburn 1314
'I Mak Siccar'

The painted scene depicted the interior of the monastery in question. In the foreground, a purple-caped, helmeted male raised a long dagger to strike another male, fallen against a table with spilt wine goblets, and lifting an arm to ward off the blow. To the right and left, monks held back amongst the pillars; also lurking, to the right, was another man with mail headgear and a long dagger.

Certainly a graphic image for a public space, albeit a side alley. It was no surprise that people might stop and stare. And lo, it was unscarred by graffiti. The only odd thing was how the young twosome, in lashing rain, had seemed to zero in on the site; as if touching base, or checking something.

As for 'the Bruce', James was well acquainted with the spider in the cave, the web, etc., but knew nothing of the violent drama colouring this old passage. The newspaper article about the student's murder came to mind on re-reading the scroll, as Alan, as he now knew him to be, had been discovered lying in *Friars' Vennel*.

Ancient Greek, yes, but Gaelic stood wholly outside James' linguistic repertoire. At best therefore, '*I Mak Siccar*' suggested 'I make succour', which made little sense. The archives was clearly in order. At worst, more grist for the pen.

"*I made sure.*' Virtually identical to the English." Sandy threw James' query back almost directly, laughing. "Guess you coming hame in 2016 gives new meaning to 'accessory after the fact'!"

"Huh? Not sure…"

"'Sir Roger', a 'Kirkpatrick', his Yankee progeny, returned to the scene of the crime!"

An involuntary shiver, then James laughed too. It was spooky. So struck was he by the dark history in the graphic tableau, he'd suppressed the name of the co-conspirator hitting 'clean-up' in the monastery. *Go you Kirkpatricks!*

"Odd you should pop in with that one – well, not really, as you're from away. Half the town's likely never passed down that alley, let alone knows its violent echoes… though just the other day, some students came by, on about the weapons in the assassination. '*What were they, where could one see or find some?'*. I'm guessing you heard about the awful recent murder there…"

James thanked Sandy and warned her to stay out of dark alleys, then proceeded directly to one himself. Namely, the *Globe*, newspaper in hand, to indulge in a pint and a crossword.

***

It wasn't so much the picnic promised in jest, as further time spent with Persephone that nudged James the next morning into detective mode; all he needed was a dingy, off-street, second floor office, a wise-cracking, chain-smoking secretary, and black and white film…

Back in the present, he'd often pondered, when dealing with his fee-paying detritus in court, on what led to the original arrest: pure intuition, Sherlockian genius, a stumble, then a gasping confession?

But no true detective begins his prowl without an 'Americano' and a legitimate omelette, both of which he knew could be had at *Pumpernickel*. A parallel motive was a gut sense he should dally further at the scene of the crime; get a feel for any lingering 'vibes'. The visitation by the passing teens in the previous day's downpour helped prick that sense.

He mused whether the historical site had already become the ubiquitous 'shrine', drawing friends and gawkers to strew flowers and pubescent messages? Lord knew, such popular reverence proliferated elsewhere, especially back in the States – though there they boasted the endless murders to stoke the vogue. As James arrived today, however, no floral or other tribute laced the wall in *Friars' Vennel*.

By his second coffee, an emerging link stamping both the Bruce's violence and Alan Sanderson's death had grown highly suggestive – as indeed it must have, James allowed, to police and the media. But he remained keen to raise his own queries.

Were the 'pageant' on the wall, the period weapons, and the venue, all the merest, wild coincidence – *no*, surely not in this small town wreathed in the fumes of centuries. Then, was the dramatic act meant to *widely* impress, make the proverbial 'statement', a perverse orchestration of some demented pedagogue, driven to teach the world a thing or two about 'natural justice'? And, as James strayed from the forensic into fantasy, perhaps serve as the first 'lesson' channeling a Ripper vein, leading to a local massacre evoking Culloden?

Outside the box, other end of the spectrum. Maybe the crime was a more focused act, aimed at the victim and *only* the victim, broader world be damned? But again, the 'duality' aspect: two perps on the wall, two weapons in each murder, two perps loose in Dumfries. And then, of likely no substantive relevance, but still colouring perceptions, the youthful *pair* paying their respects in the downpour?

James bit into a second order of raisin toast, making mental note to atone by swimming extra hard that afternoon. One other tendril nagged: the *I made sure* declaration, or family motto it would appear. It still tingled that it was kin, a 'Kirkpatrick', in aid of the wine-splashed slaying; but that phrase, or something like it, he'd heard somewhere recently, and couldn't retrieve the context.

The day's first sun gilded the café windows and turned his eye. On cue, the same girl as yesterday, though now not drenched, walked very slowly past *Pumpernickel*, this time alone. Whoever she was, she was about to assist Mr Kirkpatrick in his inquiries. James hurried to the entrance.

"Hey there. Morning. Weren't you the young lady with the thoughtful questions at my talk the other day?"

The young lady, looking more decidedly Gothic, wan and now very much the deer in the headlights, froze. Her thin lip quivered in faint response to James' cheery greeting.

"Aye..." she ventured, looking downwards.

"Would you join me for a coffee, or whatever you'd like – just briefly, if you're not due somewhere. Seeing you reminded me of some research I'm doing, and you may be the very person to help me out."

The girl looked confused, hesitant, even apprehensive, but after a few awkward seconds said, "Of course, sure... aye," and nervously followed James inside.

The shanghaied young guest quickly settled for a hot chocolate and an oatcake. James observed she might better have benefited from an entire Angus and a barrel of fries, with a side of milkshakes.

"I assume you know I'm new around here," James began opening his attempt at uncautioned interrogation. "Trying my hand at writing. I lost my wife this spring

67

(which seemed to soften the girl's gaze only somewhat) and I'm pushing my old legal self in new directions. I thought I'd be well advised to use some of my professional memories, you know, chasing justice, but in a 'novel' format – I recall one of your classmates mentioned seeking that the other day, 'justice'…?"

That snapped his subject into rapt attention.

"Geez, sorry. Rude of me not to ask my young colleague's name?"

"Abith," she repeated, as if surprised to hear it.

"Abith…?"

"Quinn, Abith… Quinn."

"Well Abith, after having a fine soup right here during the rainstorm yesterday, I happened to pass that 'Red Comyn' plaque down the lane there, er, Vennel it is. *Very* intriguing don't you think? You must have seen it sometime no doubt. I was wondering, especially after my bit at your school, as to how many locals, your friends for example, are aware of it, or know much about it. So ancient. So stark, in the middle of nowhere…?"

James dragged his last raisin crust back and forth in the strawberry jam. Quinn clearly had an answer but baulked at making it. *More info to gently prod.*

"You see – and I bet *you'd* appreciate – my story will track human behaviour, and how instructive history's lessons or critical dramas actually are, *if* ever heeded. You know, take the Red Comyn caper again, for example. What has the world learned from memorializing it, why remember it today?"

"It makes a point," Quinn finally blurted. "With the Bruce and Comyn. It... it demonstrates the value of taking action, in... in a good cause, a *right* cause... I suppose."

"Think others in your circle would agree?"

Quinn stared at her cup for a moment. "I, I don't have a 'circle'," and her eyes didn't glow so much as suddenly gleam, "... except *one* person for sure."

Seeing her grow restless, James took a final plunge. "Was that Sanderson fellow the one by any chance? Did he subscribe to some cause? Or maybe somebody feared *he* was going to take action against something...?" He had no such suspicion, but felt it useful to keep poking.

Whether Alan Sanderson had a cause or no would never have concerned Quinn, but she could certainly swear ignorance of any such inspiration. "Nae a clue, Mr Kilpatrick..."

"*Kirk*patrick, actually..."

Quinn winced slightly, but concluded, looking off like she was fingering the culprit from the witness box. "... But if he did, I can't imagine what it was. He was mean to... people, *bastard bully* since you ask. Shite to those who weren't athletes; probably kicked more heads than balls."

James took honest note of her comment, biting his lip at the unintended double entendre. She was getting edgy. He stood from their table. "I've kept you from your day. It was kind of you to lend an ear, sure we'll bump into each other again around town. Best of luck with your final year!"

"Aye. Thanks then." With that Quinn quickly shrank and scurried off like a spider to a distant corner.

James sat down again, pondering what he'd tapped into, or not. He'd been the rank amateur sniffing up the scene, and lo and behold, one of the victim's schoolmates also returned, for the second day in a row. And when queried, hadn't exactly eulogized the fellow. He admitted feeling a twinge of guilt, an adult stranger imposing on the girl, nosing about an event which would be traumatic for any young person. *Ahh, dear Pinkham's sweet love interest...* James got up once more, standing in *Pumpernickel*'s doorway for several minutes, looking up and down *Friars' Vennel*.

Not a populous lane, though at least twice the scene of infamous foul play. He could almost hear the goblet strike the stone floor of the monastery, the chilling scrape of long blade clearing chain mail and bone, the groans of agony, and the final slump beneath the table. No one to succour – indeed, with *an accomplice to* perfect the first blows.

We're alone in death... to wit, cruelly, Alan Sanderson, by chance or otherwise, in the same place and different era, by another two sets of hands. James shivered suddenly at the reflexive image of Charlie, crumpled in the hotel corridor, alone.

He went back in to collect his pen and writing folio. The table hadn't been cleared yet, and he fastened for a second on the solitary cup of hot chocolate, still half full. The residue of their exchange. Had he been too aggressive? And to what probative end?

Then he saw Sam Spade staring impatiently through the window at his table...

70

7

"Duncan! People are jumping to conclusions about that *dickheed*. There's weird questions being asked…"

"*What?* Ye've been where, Abith?"

"Down the *Vennel*, lookin' for your glasses, and he pulls me into the café and asks me stuff."

"Who's 'he'? And what's *he* know?"

Duncan, Abith's spindly desk neighbour who'd pressed James on the quality of neglected justice, lifted his melancholy visage and unbent his long limbs, ending his mirror pose of the huddled waif carved on the tombstone against which he'd dissembled for the last two hours. 1773 was the Year of Our Lord in which the relieved waif had departed this life.

"Yank barrister who gave the talk. I think he may have seen us yesterday. He was creepy, that's all. Talked about 'that Sanderson fellow'. Went on about human behaviour and sic – I dinna ken…"

They breathed intensely in a unique symbiosis, Abith and Duncan. Both were single progeny, and their respective parents hardly knew, and rarely saw them. They chose to inhabit 'history', because it was a silent, or rather, self-expressive other world, which put the present, for them at least, in its place. They hung out in kirkyards and under river bridges. They were academic stars, because such achievement did not depend on having friends or human interaction. Sex was not their bond so much as a shared outrage and horror at the world's genocidal trends, and its countless, unprosecuted evildoers.

"Think we should do something? Crowd-fund a plaque or... or memorial, or...? Make students *look* better?"

Quinn flinched visibly. "*Nothing!* Coppers'll be all down our necks. We've done nothing wrong, remember?"

"Okay, okay, but it's aye a right scunner..."

***

On his way back from the cop shop, James scouted for a newspaper and entered an imposing structure on the High Street. He was surprised for a second time that day to bump, literally, into another familiar face from his Academy debut. It belonged to a rugged lad bravely wearing a 'Chelsea FC' jersey, and commendably, also browsing in Waterstones. The youth was the antithesis of the shrinking violet he'd just left in Abith Quinn.

"Hey there, looking for a collector's edition of Blackstone's *Commentaries*?"

"Aye, sir, if Ian Rankin wrote them..."

That'll teach you, James. Why not poke a bit further with this second chance meeting?

"Heard anything more on your classmate's death?"

"Naa." He then gratuitously launched a succinct opinion of the affair. "He was a huge gawpus, typical rugby brute. Missed the national squad by not much and got into 'roids." He looked quickly at James as if to head off the next question. "I just know that, right? He was startin' to look a fair mess; word was, some *mungars* were owed big-time. Maybe they just 'eliminated' the debt…"

The theory came way out of left field, causing James to neglect raising the peculiar weapons aspect. They exchanged a few pleasantries, shook hands, and James wished him well in his studies.

***

The Globe Inn, six p.m

To her credit, Jane had yet to cringe whenever James inflicted another 'new' toast he'd picked up.

"*Ach*, ye're bleeding heather! Ye'll be cursing the Union soon enough."

"Aha! Well then, *To the King owr the water!*"

"Aye, better him than the likely next one from doon the road…"

"Hm-m, how's this one? *Damn few an' they're a' deid?*"

Jane cringed. "Right. Enough blether. Ye've earned the tour." She put down her towel to extract a huge, Dickensian-looking key and pocket flashlight from under the bar. "Follow me."

Together, they left the snug bar, crossing a tiny foyer to where Jane unlocked an intimate parlour. There was a wooden table with three chairs, panelled walls, a black metal hearth with grate, and a tall glass case in the corner with a graceful chair abutting snugly. The case held a furled ancient banner and assorted eighteenth-century china pieces, including a pitcher bearing Burns' image. A painted wood panel above the hearth depicted the young bard ploughing his father's infertile land.

"Some say the brutal labour weakened his heart for an early death…"

"Thirty-seven, right?"

"Aye." Confirmed, James thought, reflexively, as if Burns had collapsed from the carriage in front of his home just the night before. "This was his special drinking room…" Then Jane perked up with an offer he couldn't refuse. "Take that corner chair, and read me this," handing James a well-worn, folded sheet of paper, "an' I'll take your photo with that device o' yours."

James surrendered his iPad in a daze and began reading himself into history.

"Flow gently sweet Afton! amang thy green braes
Flow gently, I'll sing thee a song in thy praise…"

"Well done, laddie. Now you can tell friends and relations you sat down with the Immortal! Come, there's more."

They left the parlour to mount tight, twisting stairs off the foyer. *Right*, mused James, *Ebenezer Balfour leading poor Davie up the tower…*

Another chamber unlocked, but Jane didn't turn on any lights.

"We keep it dark to preserve the furnishings," she explained, stabbing her flashlight in selected directions. "There's where he slept it off." A canopied four-poster stood into one wall, the sheets now covered by a quilt embroidered with Burns' silhouette. Jane's torch toured the walls and small tables which held engravings and portraits, a tattered book on a small chest, and a matching bust and statuette, respectively, of Robbie and his faithful Jean Armour. Lovers still, in the dark. "He actually resided here for four months once when his farm was being fixed up."

Desecration no doubt, but James imagined himself stretching out on the bed, letting inspiration descend with the spirits...

The windows were framed by heavy curtains, which Jane now drew aside.

"See the windows?"

"Yes." But nothing twigged.

"No, here in the corner panes." So James peered closer, suddenly amazed to discern handwritten verse scratched into the glass itself, silver-white in the flashlight's glare. There were three separate passages thus inscribed.

"We've double-paned them for protection against the obvious..."

Jane shone directly on one pane and invited James to lean close and read out loud:

"There's not a flower that blooms in May
That's half so fair as thou art."

"From *Lovely Polly Stewart* in case you forgot..."
Flashlight shut off, door locked, they went back down.

"Jane, a thousand thanks. I feel like I've just been baptized!"

"Much needed I'm sure," Jane deadpanned, as she now deposited the acolyte back in the bar where the rush of conviviality sparked his appetite.

It was early in the evening, but a consecrating Scotch was assuredly called for after such a religious experience. Jane's assistant poured a double dram of Robert Burns' single malt from the Isle of Arran. "The distillery's fair new on the scene, but the whisky's fine and smoky…"

James soon tucked into a mammoth portion of halibut and chips, pausing imperiously to assess the quality of the chips, a lifelong comparative quest, being after all from Maine, when his right elbow once more produced a stranger of note. And also in uniform.

"Mr Kirkpatrick?"

James recognized the older officer from the squad car. He must have weighed at least 250 pounds, and most of it looked menacing.

"Yes, Sergeant. Can I be of some help?"

"Aye, sir, believe you already have. I'm told you're a barrister, so you'll ken we don't often make house calls to thank sources, but DCI Rodriguez advised you might be here. Wanted me to convey her thanks personally…"

"*Oh!* I… um, blind stab really. Wild hunch, maybe help eliminate a remote suspect. Just happened to see the girl twice at the scene and thought…"

"Not so blind, sir…" He eyed James' whisky, but his rugby club match being less than an hour later, more than professional ethics, quelled the urge. "*Established* an accused actually, but 'stab's not a bad word for it. Prints off the cup matched the ones on the dirk perfectly. Shouldn't say, but will tell you we haven't nicked her yet. A call has been made to her family…"

James was dumbfounded. First-time luck, sure, but he felt strangely flat when he thought of the flimsy teen in the sergeant's hands because of *his* 'hunch'. Now she was identified, he honestly found it hard to imagine Quinn capable of such violence, plunging an ancient blade in and out. Why? And what in the scheme of things had *he*, James, done?

The sergeant extended his paw courteously, and James shook it, still mute.

"Oh, and the DCI wanted me to say, 'RLS would be proud'."

8

There was Maggie by the banks o' Nith
A dame wi' pride enough
R. Burns

9:15 a.m.

Skilled flatfoot that she was, Persephone returned from her course, and had little trouble finding James down at *Scrumptious*. She breezed straight in and leaned menacingly over his second coffee.

"So, I've put you up for the 'Order of the Knights of Nith'…"

James grinned, pleased to see he hadn't been seen to 'poach' on another's turf.

"Shucks, 'tweren't nothing," he blustered through scone crumbles.

"Love to agree, but maybe I should leave town more often. You could clear my caseload."

"Ha! *Lucky is as lucky does*; that's all. To be honest Seph, I have an odd sense of guilt about the whole thing… any news on the Quinn girl?"

"Naa, apparently bit of an outlier. But we'll find her, nae bother."

"On a brighter note then officer, how was Edinburgh? Mince up and down the Royal Mile in full uniform, distracting tourists from the pipers? Tantalize underage kilts with the sheer beauty of the law?"

Much to her continuing surprise, the DCI ate up the flattery. The sandy hair, the slate, alternately intense blue eyes, shone fresh light on her world.

"Aye, last promenade I'd strut *my* admittedly superb wares on; but the National Gallery, and the green below, are always bonny. And of course, I popped into the old student pub."

"And your course, or whatever?"

"*Ach!* Bludy world's obsessed with terror. *Gee*-hadists, dashers, under every dustbin for Christ's sake. We should be more scared of Boris Johnson aping a coherent being…"

"So, a good time had by all!"

"Only stunt they didn't pull was dropping us by night without a chute into Gaza, loaded up with pretzels."

"Hmm… tread carefully, James."

"Well, we *did* blow a thousand targets to smithereens – as if I'd ever open up in a public space…"

"Ha! I know a lot of former compatriots who'd disagree. Glad to be in your cautious hands."

Persephone sat down finally, let out an exaggerated sigh, and moved to the key issue.

"Let's do dinner tonight. My treat; celebrate our new Rumpole of Galloway. The *Hullabaloo* is a great place over the Burns museum. Just over there." She pointed out the gate and across the river.

"Your devoted servant," gushed James. The Old World fairly danced with promise.

"Say, six p.m.? Sharp, as there's a chance I may have to deal with some havoc later." Persephone stood up briskly, though decidedly less motivated to return to the shop and her grim desk of late. "Gotta '*gae my bridle-reins a shake now*', adieu counsellor."

***

James spent the balance of his day once again wandering the Long Walk towards the Firth, here and there stopping at the great iron benches to repose and scribble a plot spin or disturbing character trait, and here and there to settle his conscience on ensnaring the ill-starred Ms Quinn.

At one point, he found himself engaged by an old warehouse with numerous great windows on the opposite bank. Abandoned or not, its warm, aged brick seemed to bask in the sun and the blended greenery of vines and the passing Nith. He imagined, as he habitually did whenever struck by interesting structures, a quaint law office, or now, a writer's vaulted studio; in short, he fantasized. But then, his mind free of court and client, genuine curiosity wheedled back in and he continued, bothered by what demons may have driven Abith Quinn.

An unadulterated plea for help? If so, the cry had certainly registered. A guilt complex demanding a horrible act to be duly atoned for? Not privy to the psychological mix of the soon-to-be accused, James was unable to eliminate that. Or plainer still, profound insecurity, a need to be caught and dealt with by authority?

Two theories for the killer's probable motive ultimately resonated above others: either a craving for identity, like John Hinckley; or maybe a blow struck boldly against the little person's impotence in a heartless world.

The latter held most weight, drawing on a vague recollection of Quinn's comments and those of her desk-neighbour about lax justice.

I made sure. Was Quinn the closer, or the principal attacker? Who was her accomplice?

9

By his own admission, James Kirkpatrick was a sensitive fellow, though by no means a weepy sentimentalist Tonight, however, emotion fairly danced in the Lowlands air.

The sense of lightness that followed his St Michael's visit returned, like he wasn't actually in Dumfries, seated by an amber river rushing over a weir to the sea, in sight of an *Auld Bridge* – already adopted as his personal retreat – waiting for an indisputably arresting officer to spark deadened instincts.

Romance had not exposed itself as either fact or promise since Charlie. But as James now waited, he thought of the small oval plaque on a shaded bench outside the restaurant. It was dedicated to a local couple, evidently for a love fully lived, and their countless evenings witnessing the river scene.

> *… And very near the Town*
> *The river Nith in chrystal streams runs down*
> *A pleasant bridge that's built with arches nine,*
> *Of red free stone, is stretched with a line*
> *From Vennel Foot to Gallo*way…

The 'chrystal' now threaded just *six* arches, but stood gracefully as the obvious metaphor: linking past to future, a 'bridge of sighs', 'stream of consciousness' – *very clever, James*. No question, it had become the vantage point for surveying his new life.

His head lifted involuntarily: Persephone had arrived, *before* she got there. Or so he teased her, nosing the air.

"*Penhaligon*," he said, rising. "'*Bluebell*' I bet, know it well," not adding it was Charlie's signature perfume and thus the only scent James would have recognized. "Haunting…"

Persephone kissed James deliberately on both cheeks to let him revel, then took her seat before he could pull it out and smiled, with gently probing eyes. *Of course it must be.*

"You haven't really said much about your wife – and now you have." She'd stirred some ashes but didn't want to be a mere surrogate.

James rebounded with nary a maudlin twitch. His hand reached naturally across the table for hers.

"Dear lass, no tritisms need apply. Of course I haven't forgotten, or buried my memories. But males are notoriously good at compartmentalizing. She had a creative, distinctive life, one that mattered, and, well, it's gone now, physically, but I will cherish the best of her – *you'd* expect nothing less." James smiled as deeply as he could into Persephone's self, laying emotional cards on his *tabula rasa*. "But there's no value, no reality, in swearing eternal celibacy or abstinence from life. In fact, all the more reason to *attack* the here and now…"

The most leered-at DCI in recent Scottish annals flushed with desire and a genuine sense of humanity. She was inclined to respond directly, 'Great, then let me be your first victim', but instead she held tight, because she should let his declaration hold sway.

"Male or no, I admire your philosophy, James. Flattered you share it."

She flicked her hair and blew off the wisp of dolour. "Food here's fab, laddie."

"Had a haggis-stuffed chicken the other evening…"

"James! Don't go revoltingly native on me. Ye'll want fruits of the fresh *sea* sparkling on your plate."

What James wanted was to banish the uneasiness of Abith Quinn strolling into his life. A nagging guilt punctuated his perusal of the otherwise engaging menu. He looked up; he had to ask.

"Anything to report on the Quinn girl?"

"Na, truly. But we've feelers everywhere, and as I said, seems she hung out under trestles and bridges. Campfire teen angst ye ken."

"Hmm…"

Persephone twigged, put her lager down – new-age cocktails had overstayed their Edinburgh welcome – and restrained James' drinking hand as she leaned closer.

"To be honest, *my* gut has a bad feel. I don't see this ending happily for all concerned. Never say such to the media, but I see your worry. Right?"

84

"Right. May be the defence gene in me, but I admit some vague premonition."

"Funny – well no, it's not – but I was reading *The Highlander* just the other day, and apparently in feudal times, each baron in this region had his own gallows for hanging men, and *pits* – imagine – for drowning women. Some say they were drowned as a more lenient, less violent death… why am I drivelling on like this? I wish no one ill."

"Guess there was no public defender back then, uh?" James chipped in.

"Ha! There *were* public gatherings at a 'moot hill', then the lucky damsel got tossed into what our own Sir Walter Scott called the 'deep eddy'."

"Ha, yourself. '*Boot* hill' *we* called it." Yet at this James' brow unfurled.

She was right. The Rosser West scallops, escorted by a crisp *Reisling*, slid down to smooth his pangs. Soon the pair laughed freely as they duelled with favourite passages and epigrams from their common affair with antiquity.

"… And speaking of 'law and order' counsellor (which they weren't) consider the accused, Socrates."

"Ahh, born too late! The case I missed."

Persephone's eyes narrowed.

"And your defence?"

"'Democracy should never fear minds…'"

The law leaned back in mock derision.

"Let me stab a right-ish pin in that. Context is everything, as ye well know. And the Athens of 399 BC rocked with a series of natural disasters; the gods were displeased. A Cambridge professor, Cartledge I think, holds that Socrates' state criticisms constituted what we'd now call terrorism, and his trial and conviction were legally just."

"You mean, communal good, public safety, 'national security', etc. Rings a recent bell…"

Bizarrely, a bell rang, but sonorously, and from outside. Persephone chimed in on the final strike.

"Eight bells. Friars Kirk, up at the square. Rings four times a day. That was the ancient curfew, to remind us of 'the wonder of the incarnation of Our lord Jesus Christ'."

"So, do *you* wonder?"

"Hmm, I wonder where He or She is when I clean up a battered spouse, a wasted young druggie puking in a back lane, or see a news clip of a Syrian infant shredded by a barrel bomb without prior consultation…"

"Well said, dear heart. Think maybe we're at the Irish Mist stage", and James cued a server.

"Aye merrily, Davie lad." Yet then a second bell rang. Her police mobile. She leapt up, kissed James fleetingly, leaving a buzz on his mouth, and flew out under hasty regrets.

"Sorry. Was absolutely delightful. The mess I anticipated…"

James trailed her to the entrance. The sun had been down a while but he was able to see Persephone streak over the Edwardian footbridge to a squad car already racing in. The occasion, and his new life in general, had been so convivial he'd quite forgotten the random nature of street trauma.

86

James paid the tab but chose to linger over the liqueurs already ordered. On a whim, he darted into the Gents. He was rewarded with a paper cup which he filled surreptitiously with the Irish Mists back at the table, and not wanting the evening to end just then, transported it elsewhere to savour. A hundred or so metres.

To midships of the *Auld Bridge* (he refused to call it *Devorgilla* bridge, preferring in his mind's ear the drawl-like sound of 'auld'). In the chilly night air, he warmed his innards from the paper cup, toasting the romantic bravura of first steps taken. He surveyed the scenario of his new life. There remained little doubt this would be his new domicile: an ancient estuary, solid sandstone, the proximate sea, an endless fount of custom and history prompting frequent single malts to decipher.

James let stray thoughts and the flow beneath gradually mesmerize him. He smiled as he suddenly pictured Alec Guinness in the quiet jungle evening, leaning pensively over the rail of his new-finished bridge on the Kwai river.

Then some largish object jammed into the edge of the caul caught his eye.

Something irregular, and as with Guinness, James became increasingly unable to dismiss it without further examination. He moved closer to the Whitesands end of the bridge, where the horizontal bar of the dam slanted in, to gain a better view. Within seconds, there was little doubt as to the need to resolve the anomaly, which, in its back and forth wash, seemed to beckon darkly.

James came off the bridge, clambered down the old steps off the street, through a scrub clump, and proceeded to step gingerly onto the weed-slimed stone bar, thigh-deep against the cascading, frigid water. *Jesus, man, what in hell are you doing out here!*

It took two full minutes to reach the object, by then clearly insinuating its true nature. A body, a female with neon-streaked spiked hair, clad only in jersey, jeans, and leather vest, repeatedly folded and unfolded from the fetal position. It was snagged by a branch stuck below the bar.

James struggled to disentangle the woman, finally just snapping the branch to avoid being swept over himself. As he freed the body, it swung over the falls, nearly taking him with it; in that, he realized he'd never complete the mission if he fought the surge, so let his burden ride freely atop the rush, and slowly pulled her by the feet along and against it for what seemed ages until he reached the bank.

Unaware of anything else, James heaved the body onto a flat boulder; not till then could he brush aside the sodden hair and reflexively vomit. Abith Quinn, her china pallor even more Goth.

"How's it gaan?"

James' head jerked up. A codger of the classic sort was crooked over the railing above.

"Wha – *call the police!*"

"Yer fishin', I mean. An' how'd ye geit sae drukit?"

This was surreal. James yelled, "Someone up there? Police, call the police!"

He didn't want to abandon Abith, but was about to when two teenage boys with their intrepid devices leaned over to advise that police and ambulance were on their way. James, in a daze, turned back to survey his 'catch'.

He knew better than to disturb, and obviously he'd already relocated the corpse, but a hasty peek left James unable to ignore a small wad stuffed into the laces of her Doc Martins. On pure reflex, he extracted it to reveal a tightly folded scrap of notepaper, so compact its interior inked message had not blurred with the outer moisture.

No additional light was necessary. The moon and stars, sadly, were resplendent. Block letters shouted an effort to keep control and be extra clear:

POOR DUNCAN. CARED SO MUCH, HURT SO MUCH. HE LISTENED TO ME, BUT HAS NO GUILT
   Abith Q.

An odd remorse, encased in icy reality, shot through James. How pathetic, fingering her co-conspirator by trying to exculpate him. *The poor girl didn't realize affection has no advocate in court.* Duncan had to be her Academy desk-mate, and most likely, James deduced, her rainy-day companion down the *Vennel*.

A massive lone cloud rolled in to sheath the moon and James' unconscious pocketing of the sad little testament. A mental note to pass it to Seph sailed with the cloud's passing. A squad car and ambulance shrieked in above, and the reluctant witness welcomed a pair of young male constables to his soggy perch. James gave a spontaneous but succinct recounting of his experience calculated to prompt minimal questioning. The constables, grateful for a neat narrative, and perceiving a cooperative citizen, let him trudge slowly back to the *Clog and Thistle* after agreeing to 'pop round the station' next morning, 'at yer convenience, sir, all dried out!'

A hot shower, and James sank into bed with the revelation his adopted 'hame' had become a more complex scape.

10

A light but insistent rapping on his door finally woke James. It wasn't America, so, though dozy, he didn't hesitate to open it.

"Yer nabbed."

"What…?"

Persephone stood in the muted hall light, decked out in full SWAT gear, including sidearm.

"James Kirkpatrick, I'm arresting you on suspicion of needing massage therapy, as administered by the law." Then, leaning forward in an admonishing whisper, "Seems you've immersed yourself in local matters, again…"

Heedless of his T-shirt and boxers, James was speechless. "Uh, um…" was all he mustered.

"A thorough search of the premises and your person – do I need a warrant?"

A smile broke through his torpor and James made an effort to engage the repartee.

"No, no, I'll show you everything."

"So will I. For Christ's sake, *let me in and close the door!*"

Once inside, the officer doffed her helmet, dropped the flak vest and pinned the suspect against his own door.

Then she kissed him with a surge that swept away any resistance. Her shirt fell to the floor, she unclipped a peach-coloured lace bra, bent over to shuck her panties and boots. By the time she stood, her luxurious breasts and hardened nipples blew James' sleepiness into fierce arousal. An incredible, naked woman, wearing a gun belt.

"Officer, your weapon…"

"Needed it. Was that kind of situation."

"But it's still on you – what if it goes off?"

"Be the best bang you ever had…"

That was it. As they joked afterwards, it was 'love amongst the ruins', the passion of Aeneas and Dido, Caesar and Cleopatra, and so on… conquering past losses and heroes, writhing to inhale the fresh winds of romance.

At five twenty, Persephone's mobile chimed in, as ever. James couldn't believe he was digging through bed covers for a gun.

"To be continued, my Yankee rover," she said with a hug, "gotta be up, up, and awa'."

James tottered back from the door through tendrils of '*Bluebell*', and collapsed into bed. It seemed just minutes before his door sounded a second time. *Scrooge. A second lovely apparition?*

Not quite, and it was seven fifteen.

"Do, do ye remember me?" came a voice in a flat, despairing tone.

The amorous afterglow slowed James' faculties.

"I… don't quite…"

The tall, spindly young caller, in ragged sweats and filthy sneakers, averted eye contact as he recited name, rank and serial number.

"Duncan Shaw..." Ah yes, that reedy voice. "The Academy, you talked to us..."

"Yes, yes, I remember, come in, I guess..."

They remained standing, facing each other.

"Can't find Abith," he blurted as if James should know who Abith was or that he would care for her whereabouts. "I'm, uh, needed by the police, I ken. Going to the station, but will you go with me... please. You know this stuff."

No lovely apparition for sure, but a ghostly wad of notepaper fluttered guiltily above Duncan's head. *Jesus, never handed it over to Seph!* He didn't waste time asking how he'd been traced to the B&B, but got Duncan a glass of water. Because it was all he had to offer, and because Duncan looked desiccated. Then he slipped on a modicum of clothing, sat the kid down, and pumped him gently for any background.

***

DCI Rodriguez had nipped into D&D's Pantry on Andrews Street for her morning savoury and whole milk cap. Despite a dreamy buzz from her midnight tumble, for some reason she felt vicariously distracted. After two sips, intuition suggested a wider exposure to local crime might chill James' emigre zeal. He *was* a seasoned barrister, but she understood his flight from grief and admired his plunge in new directions.

By nine fifteen, when James appeared at the station with a blanched Duncan in tow, requesting her specifically, Persephone had devised corrective diversion.

"Chief Inspector, this young man has asked me to accompany him. He's not certain precisely what you intend, but he wishes to surrender in the proper manner. I assured him you'd do the right thing in any event. And Duncan, you understand I'm not your solicitor, but if you do need someone to talk to later, I'll be around…"

Everyone looked blankly at everyone else for an instant before Persephone took over, trying hard to be professional, if not astounded. Who was this string bean juvie, besides vaguely familiar?

"Thank you, Mr Kirkpatrick. Anything more to tell us before we get on with it?" Whatever 'it' might be.

"I believe a visit by Duncan here to your fingerprint people would be productive. I think you should also know, up front, as he has urged me to advise you, he did nothing physical to actually cause death, but felt cajoled, if you will, into adding, um, certain abuse after the fact."

Now the lights went on, and the DCI continued to sit on her astonishment.

"Anything else you wish to add Duncan, while Mr Kirkpatrick is still here?"

The shell formerly occupied by an intense young academic, Duncan Shaw, stared off in bewildered resignation. "Na, naa… just wondrin' what Cambridge would have been like."

The imposing sergeant who'd pegged James in the *Globe* entered the foyer at Persephone's gesture, and steered Duncan off down a long corridor. She turned over her shoulder and mouthed, with a marvelling glance, 'the *Globe*, five'.

***

The Globe Inn
5:15 p.m.

"Hey, gorgeous." James looked up from Jane's best bitter.

"C'mon counsel, this ain't *Joe's Bar and Girl*. I prefer 'Inspector', creates more sexual tension." Yet she kissed him quickly nonetheless. "Car's just up on English Street, let's go."

"Go?"

"I mentioned therapy last night, remember? Well, I've got the pivot for your shenanigans. Taking you hame laddie, to your ancient, veritable pile. Will give life to that scene down the *Vennel* that's on your mind. And how peaceful but inhabited you'll find the place. C'mon now."

11

The past must echo in your memory
R L S

An easy, though expectant silence wreathed the couple in the DCI's classic TR4 (James all but proposed on being introduced to it) as they spun north, top down, tracking the River Nith up the A76 – 'Burns Heritage Trail' – threading dark stands of giant conifer, broad fields, rich green, gold and autumn-misted. The fields swept northwest into great rolling hills moistened by a constant-moving brush of cloud and shadow trailing teal, periwinkle and violet. Here and there, snow splashed the peaks, gradually gilded in the lowering sun.

She knew their destination, he didn't.

"*So-o-o*. 'Closeburn', my true 'hame' as you quaint locals say. And here I laboured under the illusion a *Dumfries* graveyard held my family seat: 'James Kirkpatrick, spirit merchant', enriching the sod of St Michael's not ten yards from the Immortal…"

"Aye, but that's modern, ken, eighteenth century-on, your more recent betters. We're bound for the Middle Ages, where your upwardly mobile, loyal, murderin' ilk first squatted. In fact, it's the oldest still-inhabited Scottish castle, a wee bit below Closeburn actually. *Hmm*, here's the turn now, on the right." They peeled off down a fenced lane that fell away again to the right after several hundred metres, where Persephone halted in front of a country kirk.

They left the car in the lane, no one in sight, and Persephone unlatched and pushed open the heavy black iron gate. James felt the soft wind of centuries lifting, fully expecting William Wallace to rush from the thick grass to challenge his intent.

The church, evidently in current use – posters for 'Our Harvest Home' papered the entrance arch – was itself ancient, but standing at its rear on a gentle downward slope, and then on another terrace perhaps six feet lower still, were several ruined walls and archways from far-distant times, lingering to protect a small cemetery.

"Remember the *Vennel* wall?" Persephone pointed up at identical stone crests centering three different arches. "Here, here, and there…" Each featured a hand thrusting a dirk into the air. With varying legibility, each was wrapped with the motto, *I mak sickar*. "Look close, on the sides of the blade."

"Jesus, drops of blood. Pretty graphic."

"Indeed, laddie. You know the story: the Bruce upbraiding – classy word that – the Red Comyn for betraying their alliance against Edward I. Rage ensues, Robert stabs the traitor in the Friary, exits, then doubts his blow has done the job, whereupon his pal Sir Roger flies back in and dispatches the wounded rival."

Sins of my fathers.

"Here's the positive spin, James. The crest trumpets the call to duty, and the blood marks the deed done;

shocking, but admirable just the same. *Noblesse oblige.* Otherwise, why perpetuate that dark night?"

James' aimiable guide then moved off on her own, leaving him to prowl. She killed ten minutes or so then returned.

"Well, what d'ye think o' it? M'self, I'm dying to say 'a Connecticut Yankee in King...', but you get my drift. Here's where your Sir Roger Kirkpatrick held sway in the early fourteenth century. His kin wandered over from Ireland in the eight and nine hundreds, faithful to the charms of Saint Patrick, pruned their Christian sect from a 'kil' to a 'kirk', and so you have your name, sir... these remnants were the family chapel, and if you look through those woods below the gravestones, and beyond that across the short sunken field, once a moat, you see the tower that was your Kirkpatrick seat."

James proceeded down to the terrace and leaned against the stone wall edging the sacred ground; from there, he looked back to ponder the garden of his genes. Again, Persephone held back a piece.

Such physical proximity to my heritage – if Charlie hadn't... if I hadn't walked into the Globe. The atmosphere was markedly different here in open country, few echoes of clash and clamour, more conjuring of the laird and son stalking deer and pheasant, the rough-tartaned family bundling into the chapel on a chill morning, perhaps to celebrate Easter, perhaps to commit to the very green on which he now stood, an infant taken by some as-yet-unfathomed illness...

Persephone kissed him behind one ear before James noticed her, so engrossed was he in trotting down imagined corridors.

"Well, Sir James! Let's move along to your stately pile – the tower that is – and then, I've a bold tryst to propose." A solicitous Persephone paused to put her arms around the rapt voyeur from behind, rocking gently. "So tranquil, yet tingles below the surface, aye... so, so *settling...*"

"Whew! Thought I was being taken into custody."

Rather than return to the car and lane, they clambered over the stone wall and walked directly through the narrow strip of woods into the ages-dry moat. A further hundred metres across that field, and they mounted a distinct elevation to the tray of land rooting the surviving tower of Kirkpatrick Castle.

Since 1232 AD its adjuncts had been burned or ransacked; that said, the stone tower still rose impressively, several feet thick, and according to Persephone, had been suited up internally to accommodate eight persons in period splendour. Spidering off one corner was a single-storey stone outcrop, apparently added for more modern, extended residence by the current tyrant.

There were no signs of life, so the two visitors boldly trespassed, peering in windows and sniffing the environs. It was indisputably a gorgeous day, with the waning autumn sun highlighting the surrounding panorama: thick forest to the east and south of the estate, an island of conifers to the northeast, and back over the just-toured chapel and miles beyond, the snow-capped hills in the northwest.

James raised his arms and gazed grandly about in genuine wonder.

"Why would you *ever* leave here to go into town to kill a friend's rival?"

"But that's just it, lad. For a *friend*, loyalty; *fetus amicus*, your clan's signature virtue. In fact, Sir Roger later hid the Bruce in a wooded hill not far from here till he emerged for a victory at Bannockburn."

James looked back at the tower.

"And we're still providing accommodation."

"That's the spirit, not a bad segue. And here's the deal: two weeks' stress leave – you will attest to my exhaustion…" Persephone struck a maudlin pose, "and you've been selected to oversee my rehab by way of a journey."

"Your devoted servant, I'm sure," laughed James, absolutely without a clue. "Journey?"

"Short spin southwest to Balcary Bay, my own hideaway. Special hotel with great food and wine, dangerous hikes along the Solway cliffs. You'll love it, a couple of idyllic days and then, *then*, your beginner's touch will be enlisted, with my complete confidence, in a search for closure on a… well, classic cold case shall we say. Out on the edge of the Irish Sea, at Cairnryan. My family, or really, me, has avoided this for decades – are you in, Jocko?"

For answer, James enfolded Persephone in an extended hug. He felt like a triumphant teen, bright

100

prospects in all directions, clasping his prize, as they stood ankle deep in gold autumn leaves and cow flaps, under the skeptical gaze of a multitude of sheep.

They took the lane for a pensive stroll back round to the chapel and the car.

Minutes later, Persephone whisked them into Thornhill for a light supper at Thomas Tosh, a bright, high-ceilinged structure with an open interior balcony that suggested a converted town hall. The cheerful café featured crafts, curios, books and a country kitchen that sat its patrons in the midst of the eclectic array.

Through the delight of velvety butternut squash soup and a gardener's pie with sweet potato mash, the DCI let down her hair by sharing a brief sketch of her family's bewilderment over bizarre events spun in the final days of WWII.

James quickly fell in with her blending of professional zeal and genuine sense of loss.

PART III

The weeping Pleiads wester
And I lie down alone
A. E. Housman

12

December, 1944

Thomas Gunnarsson was bitterly deflated when the Canadian Army twigged to his true age. Early in 1943, he'd presented himself to the recruiting officer in the local hotel in Vernon, British Columbia, as what a *Boys' Own* tale would have cast as a strapping young fellow. He was six feet one inch, muscled, and keen; he was also fifteen at the time.

He easily managed to make it through basic training, and was promptly shipped to England. By dint of an outdoors, mountain childhood, he was an exceptional shot, soon selected and trained as a sniper and tagged to sail for Sicily with the Canadians in June, 1943 – until a censored birthday letter from his distraught mother betrayed his age. They let him stay in uniform, but sent him up to Scotland to work along the coast, cutting timber and labouring on naval piers and military installations.

As it happened, the young patriot's chagrin soon evaporated on the shores of Solway Firth. The background hills, dense regal forests, and the brash esprit of local girls captured his senses. With a difficult childhood behind, he resolved never to return home.

In December, 1944, Thomas and three other robust teens were transferred from Auchencairn to Stranraer on

Loch Ryan, a coastal enclave two miles wide and seven and a half long that emptied into the Irish Sea. There they worked on additional construction and maintenance of Cairnryan Military Port. A principal feature of the latter was its mammoth, log-built quay running more than 500 metres along the northwest stretch of the loch at Cairnryan. Thomas took immense pride that the key timber was Canadian.

The four lads were billeted in an eighteenth-century merchant's house in the village, directly up from the quay; which was a boon, as the other labourers were mostly shunted into 'dormitory' rail cars on a track siding back in Stranraer.

In April, 1945, a serious gash on his left arm, courtesy of an errant saw blade, placed Thomas in the care of a precocious and equally young volunteer nurse from Lockerbie. Jean's duties at a converted inn just outside Stranraer were dedicated to restoring seriously wounded Commonwealth front-line soldiers. Thomas Gunnarsson, however, she treated as if he'd been winged by a German machine gun while single-handedly destroying an entire pillbox.

There was not a carnival of things to entertain one in any conventional sense in this reach of Scotland, but the pair were heedless of such, quickly growing inseparable. Their russet and sandy heads were routinely visible wending up from the coast road through farm fields, to the upper pastures with cows and sheep, past grouse and stags scuttling in and out of the cool woods, walking and talking passionately about the future. Thomas never forgot the road sign, angled as if by the wind towards their upward trek: *Little Laight, Lairdshill, Bonniebraes.* A rich cluster of Scottish lingo, but he cherished the first name because he joked that Jean was only a 'little light' when he carried her piggyback up the steeper grades.

Invariably, they halted at a commanding prospect, a smattering of deserted stone foundations looking westerly out the loch's ocean mouth towards Belfast, just barely out of plain sight. The grassy space between the giant gnarled roots of an aging oak made the perfect bower for two snuggled humans.

Gazing out, Jean would tease Thomas for a deficient literary background. 'See over there, that's Loch Ryan Lighthouse, built by Alan Stevenson ye ken, Robert Louis' father – *what!* You don't know *Kidnapped, Treasure Island?* Shame, oh *shame*, my sweet Canuck! But someday soon, aye, ye'll take me out to *my* treasure isle – no mind we're young. Only a few kilometres off Land's End, they say, down the right. Was a hideout once, for pirates and religious fugitives – aye, we'll have to update you on that as well – never been of course, but seen pictures of it. Tiny, craggy, velvety green, a lady told me it looks like a beehive fallen upside down into the sea. No one lives there now but puffins and seals. D'ye ken Thomas, we'll start our own colony there, loads of time to read and read!'

Throughout the summer following V-E Day, the loch witnessed a growing flotilla surface in its bright waters. By late autumn, some seventy-five U-boats from Hitler's Wolf Pack had been escorted in to surrender at the military port, many lashed together back at Cairnryan, there to be unburdened of their crews. Thomas frequently paused on the pier to watch the eighteen to twenty men in German uniform assemble on deck for a final time, then be marched off into detention. Most looked no older than Thomas, and many were smiling; he could only imagine why they looked relieved, not humiliated.

As the vanquished departed, naval experts hustled down the conning towers to scour the bowels for any technical innovations or illuminating logs. In due course, British destroyers towed the silent hulks, six to eight at a time, out to Bloody Foreland off Ireland's northwest coast, and blasted them with their guns until they sank a thousand fathoms to the Atlantic floor.

With this protracted inundation of former enemies and their munitions, security around Cairnryan's quay in particular was heightened. As a result, Thomas had to follow more regimented hours, including periodic sequestering, finding himself snatching trysts with Jean in brief windows of evening time. Love found its ways in all manner of storage sheds, outbuildings and forest bowers.

In late October, however, a combination of Jean falling prey to a mysterious hospital infection, and a two-week security clampdown at Cairnryan for James, put a crimp on their amorous contacts. The last three U-boats were due in during this spell, one of them a real prize as it was reputedly an advanced Elektra, type XXI, as opposed to the workhorse Atlantic VIIC/41. Its skipper, Kapitanleutnant Erwin Christopherson, was pegged to be a unique repository of intel on high-level Nazi technology, as well as being a survivor, a credible rapporteur on Admiral Canaris' strategy.

The net effect was nearly a month without romantic contact. In late November, Thomas, at last sprung from duty, raced into Stranraer. But there was no Jean to greet him at the rehab centre. He was told by the matron she was missing, and had not been seen for over two weeks. Did *he* know anything? Jean had been 'distraught' about something extremely personal. The authorities were immediately alerted, and Thomas was questioned severely, but his laudable military involvement soon killed any hue and cry for 'the boyfriend' to be charged with something. No relations – Jean had never mentioned any to him, or indeed, to Red Cross officials – ever materialized.

The final, 'prize' sub was dragged back out to sea early one morning and blown to bits off a small uninhabited island. It wasn't clear to locals whether its shorter passage to a graveyard just off the bottom of the Ayrshire coast was by way of respect, or just the Navy's fatigue in sailing all the way to Bloody Foreland anymore. Thomas was demobbed almost immediately afterwards, stripped of his military cocoon and budding romance. But faithful to Jean and earlier intent, chose to stay on in Scotland, though nowhere near Loch Ryan.

Within days, in a small pub, he met another Canadian vet, an affluent one who'd apparently treated himself to a victor's sojourn at Trigony House, a picturesque estate just outside Dumfries, more or less midway between Closeburn and Thornhill. Thomas summoned all that was energy in his bereft soul, caught a bus, and presented himself to the proprietors the following day.

He determined to change his surname, personally, not officially, to Armour, and under such moniker, favourably impressed the management and was immediately hired as estate groundskeeper, with a tiny cottage at Trigony's rear.

As the years passed, he slipped benignly into history and further anonymity. Over the same period, the police books in Stranraer remained open but inactive as no one ever produced anything meriting active pursuit of the young nurse's disappearance.

13

Balcary Bay Hotel, Auchencairn

They wheeled through the gate in the late evening, after some two kilometres winding down a tree-covered lane from the old village of Auchencairn. A two-storey, robin egg's blue and white cottage structure curved firmly but gracefully around the northerly rim of this inlet on the Solway, with lush greenery and scaping tucking it into the tide-wash below. Straight out, smack dab on the near horizon, a symmetrical green hump formed an island 'plugging' the two corners of the bay. *Where have I been?* thought James. Rustic, yet luxurious in promise – and all in the tow of Persephone!

The woman at the front desk didn't blink at their late arrival; she ushered the pair directly into the salon, flickering warmly with a great fire, its main windows facing on the hilly island and the great wash of inky blue before it. A plate of exotic cheeses, biscuits and chocolates, and two fine Scotches, appeared without asking. Breakfast from seven til nine thirty; wonderful to see you again, Inspector.

Typical of James in any new setting or adventure of consequence, he was up at dawn to scout the new environs, even with his sylph still smouldering in the sheets.

At Balcary Bay, any scouting began with prowling the sweep of sand and shells at low tide. First James headed southeasterly, to the weathered oyster nets and poles staked out towards the 'hill' island, now known to him as Hestan, then back along the hotel's front, bending gently into the bay's south-western rim, marked dramatically by a marvellous faux castle home standing sentinel against the distant, opposite shore of the Solway.

Kicking the sand, raking the shells with his fingers, smelling the rich salt air and wrinkled kelp – Persephone was still sprawled in bed – James inhaled the tranquility exhaled by nature's grand rhythm. After an hour, he parked himself in the sand under a thick clump of ivy and gorse, stretched out and just gandered.

After a few minutes, a mild gust of wind, and a slight motion off to his right drew Robinson Crusoe's casual attention. A woman, perhaps in her sixties, well booted and scarved for her quest, meandered into sight and passed in front of him. Shell-seeking obviously, but not in the desultory tourist mode, but more intensely.

"Sorry, I got all the good ones," James volunteered cheerfully from his little burrow.

The woman smiled without looking up or stopping.

"But did you get a pelican's foot?"

She paused when James rose and approached her with genuine curiosity.

"A long time ago, when I was a wee girl, I spent countless happy hours here collecting. Especially periwinkles, whelks, and very rarely, pelican's feet."

"What exactly would I be looking for, then?" James asked, immediately dropping his head and scrutinizing the miasma of sand, stones, and all kinds and sizes of shells and amber weed.

"A wee conical shell, with a kind of 'spatula' extending off one end. A flat bit, like a web foot."

"Aha! And what are my chances this morning?"

"Not brilliant, even for a novice American." The woman winked. "I kept all mine from childhood in a jar of water – still have them, but the water's gone..."

And so was she, rapidly outpacing James in her skilled quest for yesterday. James straightened up and smiled. There were worse things to do early in the morning on a Gaelic coast.

There's a metaphor here... but then he grounded it, straining to find a pelican's foot on his way back up to poached eggs and croissants with Seph. Fine fuel for their promised hike.

***

By yon bonnie banks and by yon bonnie braes...
R. Burns

They escaped the dense pines piping the shoreline cliffs, not breathless, but breathing freely. A narrow track ran on and upwards over grassy summits, tracing a westward series of precipices that sliced into the wider expanse of the Solway.

Above the giant gannets and wheeling gulls, and the waves shattering below into creamy lime, everything fell silent. One of those moments and vistas that pull onlookers together, and at the same time, outward. Into realms of reflection too often neglected.

Balcary Bay indented behind them to the left, with quaint Hestan Island corking its mouth, and directly south, across the Solway in the distance, large hills ribboned the horizon in a filmy, cornflower blue. A row of wind turbines planted in the sea fronted the coast like a flashing picket fence. The white-gold effect in the late afternoon sun was surprisingly esthetic.

James stopped at one point to peer giddily down the chimney between two crags. In an instant, he morphed into young David Balfour, scrambling upward behind the iconic Jacobite, Alan Breck, fleeing the English.

His fellow scrambler patiently observed the imagination in flight.

"Sorry. Lost in boyhood," James admitted after several minutes, flushed.

"And why not. Life's short, ye ken?"

James clasped Persephone by the shoulders, looking anxiously into her fresh complexion and blown hair.

"Can we make the glen before the Red Fox?"

Persephone matched his earnest face, leaning close and whispering. "Aye. But, *how green the grass is all about! We might as well sit down,* and tap that flask you tucked in your pocket."

"Something poetic in your words, Dear Officer."

"Should be. My fave, A. E. Housman."

"Stellar. Let's 'take to the heather' then, back from the edge."

Out came the flask and several healthy swigs, while the pair stretched out to absorb the horizon in silence.

"*Ah-h-h...* but shouldn't *we* utter something profound to mark the occasion?"

"The occasion?"

James gave it due consideration.

"Of delighting in the obvious, the tangible earthly joys we ignore every day." And then, inspired, he added, "The fact these cliffs, the ocean's heaving yet peaceful tumult, the expanse of sky, are always out here." *Why, James?* "A vast repository for sadness and loss, and so, a great balm for the soul."

"You've been too much with Mr Burns, my son," Persephone tisked, "but, but *bludy gud*."

James feigned a smug grin. A palpable swelling in his throat betrayed genuine belief in his airy declaration.

"Hmmm. Well, that's *my* sermon from the mount – your turn, Morse!"

James' Waterhouse incarnation rolled lazily towards him. Her unbound hair was spliced with the tall, pale grass and emerald eyes danced through like a lovely Cheshire Cat.

"Housman not enough for you?"

"A veritable giant, Inspector, but it's not from *your* inner self. Come on, only the wind will know..."

Persephone took another sip then shook her head slowly, as if incredulous at her recollection.

"Aye then, a student frolic back in Edinburgh. We were at the *Greenmantle*, all pissed *drucken*, and for the first and only occasion – *ha!* – I got up on a table and started bletherin' like the wise sophomore…"

"Ye-es?"

"… And the words have remained. Don't know why, pure embarrassment maybe, but burned for some reason into my memory."

"Hurry then, I'm all ears, and I hear their horses!"

At this Persephone stood suddenly, looking westward over the great rollers below.

"… rich and influential, poor and inconsequential, all of us are, so far as we see, hear, and touch each other, present travellers, bound irrevocably for oblivion."

James sat up, dazzled. "*Jesus*, Seph! *You're* the scribe, not me. This, this is so, so damned *cool* for a bruised colonial lad, sharing muses, here on a Scottish shore." Then the very thing floated up, on fervent demand, from ages past. "Perhaps a lighter note for our journey: *But he that drinks in season, shall live before he dies.*"

The woman who'd briefly forgotten her police self, forgotten how long she'd languished 'at sea', laughed at the undulating kaleidoscope of blues below, turned from her trance and knelt beside James. *Here* was her shining 'spring'. And the projects, the streets and punters, they were *Hades*. She cupped James' face in her hands, planting her mouth to seal his lips, and kissed him as if unlocking would let the tide rush in and take the moment.

14

Balcary Bay Hotel, dining room

Persephone looked genuinely transported through her raised glass of Chablis.

"This afternoon... I'm thinkin' it was the right trick, my James."

"Meaning?"

"Meaning, up on the cliffs, staring over the firth, the gannets and cormorants floating about – sounds corny sure, but time stopped, and it could have been *any* year. Kind of sets up our 'investigation' at Cairnryan, ye ken. If *we* don't – and thanks my Yankee dearie for being part of the 'we' – finally unearth some answers, some peace for her spirit, my poor old aunt, who is by the way the subject of our quest, will haunt me forever. As a copper sure, but more as the last of anyone around to give a damn..."

James trailed a morsel of venison through the red wine sauce.

"Of course. Otherwise, we're all just proverbial dust in the wind – *so-o*, the facts, ma'am, just the facts. Give me all you have to share."

And the inspector did, visibly startled at times by her first real exhumation of a family bruised and shredded long ago.

"Best start with the Sandersons, my maternal grandparents. The paternals, of course, weren't on the scene till 1973 when Mam married, rather oddly, at the age of forty-four and proceeded to have me at forty-six, a miracle baby to be sure. They had no use for Sandersons, and after Dad died, what line there was with us went dead. They both died some time ago, never really aware of or interested in the Amelie passage – digressing aren't I?"

"Press on, Seph. I promise you it's engrossing and I'm taking mental notes like a good copper." One such mental note being this all made Persephone forty-one, and things remained feasible for children that had been denied Charlie – *and wasn't he just jumping ahead and cocksure!*

"Well anyway, the Sandersons hailed from up in Lochaber. I never met them. They had three children. A son, Robert, several years before two daughters: first Hortense, my mother, and four years later, Amelie – no idea the inspiration for either name. A very spread-out lot when you think of it, but I don't. Uncle Robert – never met him either, sounds weird even saying 'uncle' now – enlisted in the RAF day one in 1939. He miraculously survived, a Group Captain, but the family, such as it was, never saw him again. And talk about a rush to truth and reconciliation; before the end of May, 1945, he'd met and married a German girl and settled, permanently, in Hamburg. Never been back, never heard from him, not even all those years afterwards when my dad was killed. Never expressed an ounce of curiosity about Amelie…"

James offered a pause.

"Should I assume the Allied fraternizing didn't play well back amongst the heather?"

"Naa, it was more the complete schism from kin, as if erased from sight. Maybe the War obliterated family sentiment. Anyway, when he was up in the air over England's green and pleasant land, my grandparents left Mam and Amelie with in-laws in Dumfries – an aunt and uncle presumably, whom I've also never met – and went down to visit old friends in Coventry. That was 1940, so ye know how that played: they disappeared in the firestorm and rubble. A well-heeled ex-sweetheart of my grandfather arranged to plunk my mam in a fine boarding school in Edinburgh, and she eventually went on to university at the amazing age of sixteen, but Amelie... well, she just flat out vanished almost hours after being told, before any angel could intervene. Trauma perhaps. She was only eleven at the time, but a self-contained spirit. The in-laws dropped out of the recorded picture. We'll never know... complete and total mystery."

James was duly puzzled.

"But we're headed for this place, Stranraer, tomorrow, so something else *did* become known?"

The pair had by now drifted from crème caramels into the parlour and a glorious couch by the fire, where James sank down feeling decidedly blessed. An engaging woman in every way was confiding an intriguing, personal tale which flattered him accordingly, recalling countless client histories. And the late night icing, they were secreted in a unique hideaway on the Scottish coast, sipping the finest He realized he was sloughing his own shades, moving on.

119

"Aye, but it'll cost you two *Irish Mists* to learn it Sherlock…"

Persephone gathered her reflections while James nipped into the bar and commandeered the two liqueurs. She was grappling seriously with her own 'mystery' for the first time, and was forced to see how little there was actually extant for examination.

"Nothing, and I mean nothing, was heard or seen of Amelie Sanderson, by anyone known to my mother, for four years after my grandparents' deaths. The total absence of immediate family in turbulent times, and my mam's intense immersion in the girl's school, matched by the simple fact she was hardly equipped to 'investigate' anything, let Amelie essentially slip into the ether. Mam later said she got the impression no one ever actually *reported* Amelie missing; all anybody seemed to know was she had become invisible."

"Dust in the wind…"

"And no one ever learned a spec about those four lost years, where or how she lived; but then, in the late summer of 1945 – and believe me, I know it's Dickensian, the coincidence – when Mam was entering university, a roommate showed up for her tiny flat off the Royal Mile. The woman was older, as she'd been certified as a nurse before the War, and had determined to get a further degree in English Literature to 'balance her sensibilities', but had delayed higher education to spend the War as a catastrophic injury specialist in Queen Alexandra's Imperial Military Nursing Service, first at St Thomas' in London, then as a front station nurse in France and

Holland, and finally, as a 'respite' prior to demobbing, a rehab consultant out at Stranraer. When Mam shared her own background, that she was from Lochaber, her parents were victims of Coventry, and her only family an estranged older brother and a younger sister who'd disappeared, her new flatmate did a double take…"

"Whew, frissons down my neck. Forgive me, Seph, I'm being swept into some Brit war film, khaki uniforms flapping everywhere, lovely 'Bluebirds' ministering to poor lads, families pulled apart…"

"Ha! Deal with the ministering when we 'coorie doon for the nicht', but here was the first break, if you can call it that: the woman initially recalled a few conversations from her brief tour at Loch Ryan with 'a suspiciously young' nurse's aide. She seemed to her 'rather lost as an individual, though quite functional and independent'. The only personal data to emerge was an overheard response the aide made to a severely disabled soldier by way of commiseration; she apparently told the patient *her* parents were both dead, her brother probably MIA over Holland, and a sister was out there somewhere, 'God knows…'"

"OK then, a dramatic possible lead?"

"Which Mam willed to be *fact*, so she pressed the ex-nurse to dredge her memory for absolutely anything else, no matter how trivial, she could associate with the aide. A week later, out of the blue, she steps from the shower and without pause tells Mam, 'She had this boyish adventure thing, loved the idea of pirates, and I once saw a copy of *Treasure Island* in her nurse's satchel'. Mam immediately remembered how Robert's books had become Amelie's favourites, even before she was old enough to fully appreciate them."

By now, a second liqueur glimmered from the coffee table at the raconteur and her devotee, and they'd promised hotel staff to turn off the parlour lights when they eventually retired. James snapped his head suddenly.

"Jesus, Seph! A *name*! You didn't mention her name. Surely that would have been a primary verifying clue?"

"*Ach!* Sorry 'bout that, completely forgot. 'Jean Armour' was how the aide introduced herself, but it didn't dampen Mam's instincts after she heard the pirate and adventure stuff. Amelie's Robert had 'left' too, and despite her big sister's teasing, she often prattled about her dream to bear superior, 'poetic' children for Scotland. She sought to lose herself, so why not Jean Armour? – though hardly an effective cover alias for the Dumfries-Galloway district."

"So what did your mam do with her intuition?"

"She hopped on a bus to Stranraer, then literally ran into the Auxiliary Territorial Service rehab centre. The second person she encountered in the entrance hall she immediately recognized as her sister, despite her hair being stuffed under a beret and the passage of four long years. There was a reflexive embrace, then Mam was devastated when Amelie drew back, insisted on being called Jean, and made it plain she was not anxious to be 'discovered'. She'd found a lad who worked out at the military port and Mam much later wondered if he might have been tapped to become her family."

"Feels like a period BBC drama, Seph..." was all James repeated for the moment.

"She and Mam each had their paths, and had been cruelly obliged to find them. As Amelie put it, 'so we sail on separately, sister'. Mam watched, stunned, as Amelie turned and went off to help with a vet, and the two didn't even share tea. Mam retreated to Edinburgh, vowing to try again, but then, 'again' turned out to be too late when the autumn ended with Amelie's total vanishing act."

James got up slowly and went over to the window. A spectacular moon hung in a clear sky over Hestan Island; all else, sea and backdrop hills, was rolling shadow. He looked back at Persephone, arms spread along the top of the couch, lost in unfamiliar emotional sleuthing.

"And I guess I should end by mentioning Mam's no longer herself. Whatever she knew was long ago told me, and any new directions or corroboration of fresh threads is out of the question – so sadly."

Let's keep sanguine for tonight.

"Thanks to you, Seph, I'm a found Scot; not to worry, we'll crack the case, or whatever you say."

James' melodramatic soul pulled a curtain on the little scene. It positively reeked of Buchan. He smiled intently at Persephone, then let himself stare out the window again; he imagined the two of them, sliding into bed as the *heaving waves rolled on into the ink black hills*.

***

Cairnryan, November 28, 1945

He'd dismissed the land of his birth, made a new life here, and though he wasn't a celebrated war hero, he'd undeniably played a part in the grand cause. But now, this invigorating Scottish district had swallowed his Jean. Young Thomas Gunnarsson felt his heart sink to his feet, and every step taken crushed it further.

For nearly a full day after he forced himself to make a final trek to their special place above the loch, Thomas sat in a near-catatonic state in front of the old merchant's house, staring over the tides. He was rooted here for the moment, for better or worse; but he hadn't the will to think what he would do.

Late in the afternoon, Thomas let out a profound sigh and managed to speak to another human. A Chief Petty Officer was crossing over from the adjacent pier Thomas had helped maintain, leaving behind him U-2540, the grey and disconsolate residue of the Wolf Pack nightmare.

"When's she due to be towed out?" Thomas muttered.

"Uh?" His Majesty's tar was obviously intent on finding the pub. "She meets her fate 0600 tomorrow. Special ammo on the destroyer – only headed out as far as Ailsa Craig though. The top brass wants folks on land to witness it. Special occasion they're making of it I suppose…"

"Oh…"

"Cheers, lad, I'm thirsty."

Thomas looked back at the pier and the lone sub again and had a sudden, suffocating pang.

15

Cairnryan, November 9, 2016

'Auspicious' may not have been the exact word to describe James' first impression of Stranraer, but he felt strangely upbeat, imbued with purpose, as he looked across the old ferry wharves, down Loch Ryan, and fastened on its distant exit into the Irish Sea.

Nothing trite, but he deeply wished to 'come through' for Persephone. How often did a guy get a noble quest these days?

Persephone did a quick tour of the town for James' benefit: the run-down harbour, St John's Castle, Castle Kennedy gardens on the town fringe, and *The Grapes* – "solid pub, James, we'll be back...", then proceeded out the other end of town a couple of kilometres along the northerly shore to a cluster of mainly humble but venerable homes lining the water.

This last destination was Cairnryan, and Persephone had booked them, online, into an eighteenth-century inn called the *Auld Cairn*, which stood just yards up from the loch. Directly adjacent, reclined an equally aged structure bearing a weathered shingle proclaiming the *Merchant's House, Bar and Restaurant*.

"Ye're a wee bit early, but aye welcome. Think ye'll like the room." A very authentic-looking proprietess, with blonde hair, teal eyes, ruddy complexion and much sparkle, shooed the arrivals through the small entrance hall and up narrow, spiralling stairs. "We're 300 years old, but it's a cozy nook." Grinning broadly, James chuckled, much like the sympathetic woman innkeeper in the original *39 Steps*.

And the room did not disappoint. It sported a four-poster bed buried in thick puffy pillows and covers, ancient brick and stone hearth in one corner, large window overlooking the grassy path across the road below, and the slender beach running directly below it. The soft green rise of the opposite shore stretched along clearly two kilometres off.

They gave the bed a spontaneous frolic, then stood at the window afterwards, wrapped in a single sheet, watching a huge white Stena Line ferry glide by westwards in powerful silence.

"Like a surreal cloud, isn't it?" Persephone observed, dreamily. "Headed for Belfast, James – a sign maybe? Heading out, sailing on? I wonder if Amelie didn't just take off somewhere…"

"You mentioned she had a boyfriend who worked out this way; bet they walked out here, rather than back in Stranraer – wouldn't you? Why don't *we* take a stroll west before supper? Get a feel for the place and time maybe? A good dinner, sleep, then onto the trail of yesterday, *tomorrow*!"

"You're getting gud at bletherin', my dear ambulance chaser…"

***

The deep blast of a ship's horn shivered the *Auld Cairn*'s timbers and woke the itinerant gumshoes at six a.m. sharp.

"She's off for Northern Ireland," Persephone burbled. Then she threw off the duvet and sat bolt upright. "And we're off too… but *where,* James? Where would *you* start? I've dibs on the obvious, the town archives, any local police records. Go from there… and by the way, once in town, the car's with me, you'd only kill innocent people."

James listened more or less intently, nuzzling the nape of her neck, humming something indiscernible.

"James!"

"Uh… *hmm.* I think the best strategy for me is playing the stranger in these parts bit. Nose around as the hero does, see what pops up to a completely unassuming eye."

She looked sharply look down her lovely nose.

"You mean, check out all the cafés?"

"Ha! No… but not a bad idea!"

They shared a bath in the vintage claw-foot tub, then revelled in the *Merchant's House* smoked Scottish salmon and poached eggs. They were so mellow they nearly failed to make it out the door by nine thirty, when institutions would hopefully be open.

James stood at the bus station across from Stranraer harbour and waved as Persephone sped off.

"See you at *The Grapes* around two p.m., *if* you find it!"

It was midweek, so commerce, such as existed, ought to be open and active. James walked in closer to what seemed likely market or trade areas, appreciating some colourfully painted old homes and shops along the way. When he passed a street sign indicating Ailsa Crescent, he thought, *Why not*? for no reason except recalling the distinctive name of the tiny isle on the tourist map in the *Globe* back on his first night.

Nothing ventured, nothing gained!

Lo and behold, just a few doors in, a cheerful shop window framed with wrought-iron knights, kilted brigands, griffins and damsels beckoning from storm-tossed ships, invited all and sundry to peruse the cultural trove minded inside by the Stranraer and District Local History Trust. James accepted.

An intense-looking young woman with flaming, razored hair and gold nose ring, seated on a bar stool in one corner, looked up from her copy of *The Girl With the Dragon Tattoo* and offered a tentative smile.

"Not seen you here before, sir. Can I help ye?"

James spied a central display table with a lectern holding a glossy document to which an overhead arrow entitled, *Stranraer in a nutshell,* pointed. James ignored the surrounding shelves of books and glass cases guarding assorted treasures and made a beeline for the display.

"Thanks, think I should scout a bit first if that's OK?"

"Aye then, let me know…"

It was natural curiosity – he wasn't going to discover Amelie Sanderson or Jean Armour on that lectern – that nudged James to soak up several centuries of local background in a few minutes; though, it might for no particular reason be helpful to have an historical sense of local inclinations. What milieu had the lost sister/aunt flung herself into?

It appeared the Register of the Great Seal of Scotland had enshrined the entry of the 'Clashant of Stranrawer' into the Barony of Kinilt in 1596, followed by maturity as its own Royal Burgh in 1617. Notable amongst its vicissitudes was the garrisoning of English troops in the mediaeval Castle of St John in the late seventeenth century. From there, the Catholic English king brutally expunged as many Scottish Presbyterians as he could: widely known as 'the killing time' – a label vaguely familiar from one of James' recent Dumfries encounters.

Over the years, Stranraer had striven to be a key market town and transhipment venue. Sitting on the isthmus binding the Rhins of Galloway – the would-be island – to the Dumfries/Galloway district, its fortunes lifted in the 1860s with the arrival of rail linkage. More laterally, the once thriving ferry port had suffered, from amongst other factors, the relocation to Troon of a catamaran service to Ireland. Now, native industry and tourism presumably sustained some 10,000-plus good citizens.

As his eyes moved off the document, James noted the always fascinating sub-designation of regions. Stranraer was, apparently, also a part of Inch and Wigtownshire –

Wigtown'? Hey, that's home to the Wigtown Book festival, hottest new book event this side of the Atlantic! What terrific motivation for a novice, but James felt immediately guilty for thinking of his own literary ego, and refocused on his appointed task.

There was an audio shelf along one wall and, on pure whim, James inquired if there were any oral histories or personal vignettes from the Second World War era. The woman looked up, impressively attuned.

"Perhaps a relative over here in the War, looking for old comrades he or she might have known?"

"You're a credit to the Trust! Actually, a nurse's aide who was stationed here during 1945."

"Hmmm…", Alix McVey, as her name tag advised, came over to the shelf and dragged her fingers quickly along the CDs and DVDs. "Let's see… aye, ye're maybe in luck! A doctoral student from Edinburgh donated some of her research about a month ago, and I'm pretty sure it had something to do with nursing. Here it is. Good hunting, sir…"

James was shown to a comfortable-looking executive chair at a table with laptop, headset, and an antique clerk's lamp above a blank notepad and waiting pen. The DVD's spine read 'Margaret Livingstone-Bussell, Memories of WWII Auxiliary Territorial Service at Stranraer, Sept. 21, 2016'.

James activated the disk and sat back, expecting a frail form in an armchair, feeble voice lamenting the damage to 'all those lovely young lads…' He sat up quickly when he was instead greeted by a vivacious, articulate woman who

130

stood quite sturdily in the midst of what looked to be some kind of reception or social affair. She brandished a teacup and piece of cake in admirable fashion, as she leaned confidently into the camera.

'*Yes dear, I'm from Manchester originally, and never thought to wind up here, but when the ATS posted me to Stranraer, and there were endless scones, and occasionally real butter, oh my! I had to stay, and I did. And here I am at ninety-three, a Scot as far as I'm concerned, thrilled to talk to you!*'

James had always been a history buff, but his true engagement derived from experiencing the live human nexus, the magically spoken testimony of witnesses to distant, great events. Back in Maine, the prize item in his den had been a VHS tape of rare film and audio from the late 1890s, of Civil War vets from both sides – enabling him to hear a voice, *today*, sharing *personal* memories of Devil's Den and Pickett's Charge over the wheat field!

'*Oh, we did much more than just medical care. Imagine this old bat driving American lorries and jeeps off the ships when they docked here. I was twenty-one, and at war! But yes, dear, we did lose our hearts to many young men, broken, scarred, afraid – such waste, such sacrifice... We were all desperately young. Such contrast, our enthusiasm against the wreckage coming back... many of the nurses were naturals, real little saints, others crumpled and had to leave... a very emotional time it was...*'

Then came the student-interviewer's voice:

131

'Any person in particular, or keepsakes, photos, albums, that you specially hold in your memory today?'

'That was all yesterday, and should best stay there. I keep busy now with our wonderful community and anything they'll let me do... but I can always trot in to the gallery in the local museum and see the faces again, the staff, the grounds, if I feel like it...'

James put the headset down and thanked Alix, asking where the Stranraer Museum was located: he had fresh marching orders. Luck rode with him, did it not?

As it turned out, it was just a few minutes' amble over to George Street, not far from the docks, to the Old Town Hall, which housed the local museum in question. A graceful building, James noted as he looked at the spire, its attitude not unlike a classic New England church or something by Wren. Admission was, as ever, thanks to an enlightened UK, free. Inside, he again confronted a young female custodian.

"Oh! *Dear Ms Bussell!* So glad you were able to experience her; she *was* a cherished figure around Stranraer, but I'm betting you've already gathered that..."

"Was?"

"She passed away only two weeks ago, I'm afraid. Was in all the papers."

There goes a potential viva voce witness... Any photo clues were now even more crucial. James tried to remain gung-ho. It was somewhat heartening to see that everyone appeared to know everyone else around town.

"If you'll just come through to this side gallery..."

132

It was a perfectly curated, white-walled, arched enclave, much like a fortress powder chamber; the numerous black and white photos and framed newspaper clippings stood out more starkly to the viewer. James thanked his escort and let himself drift with the tide of faces and long-past context. For half an hour he all but neglected his brief, so enthralled was he in all the eager, drawn, hopeful, distant expressions thrown back at him. What had they seen, endured, what were their hopes and future? Were any still with us? And the sheer primness and rose-like glow of the nurses and aides struck James, though only in his forties, with the raw slap of youth.

Ah yes, the aides, man, your focus. There were lots of 'strawberry socials' and cheerful garden birthdays, or formal staff groupings in which aides were clearly discernible from doctors and regular nurses. *Seph's mam's roomie must be in here somewhere*; but of course, there was no verification likely since her mam had recently removed to a Newcastle home for dementia. Frustrating, as any formal staff snap with the roomie would likely have Amelie in it.

James took iPhone shots of several photos, one in particular with a very young-looking aide with her one arm over the shoulder of a wheelchair patient, and the other holding a book. Instinct promoted it as a pic of interest; Persephone would have to pass judgment.

It had been a fascinating morning for the neophyte investigator, if not productive for the cause. He fished a bit further on his way out.

133

"Anything else, or anywhere at all, you might suggest by way of digging up more anecdotal or documentary records of Stranraer in the Second World War?"

"Well you won't have to dig this up, but tomorrow as you're probably aware, is Remembrance Day, and I know several veterans may be at the cenotaph for a special ceremony. Might want to attend? Starts around ten thirty a.m."

"Thanks a bunch, miss, see if I can dig up a tie."

He exited the Hall as the cry of a lonesome pale ale wafted overhead and he began intense queries of passers-by as to the exact location of *The Grapes*...

Persephone was frank in admitting her pleasant but not very fruitful immersion in another era. Over an honest pint and a steak and ale pie at *The Grapes*, which her partner did manage to find, she reported on the substantial collection at the library and archives. Despite numerous charming personal memoirs, and extensive scrapbooks of the town in wartime, she'd found no relevant strands, and certainly, no photos or references remotely evocative of Aunt Amelie.

She'd been hopeful that a contemporary scan of police records from the War might scratch out something new, but she'd found little to enthuse about there too. At Stranraer's Police Scotland station – in 1945, the resident posse was known as the Wigtownshire Constabulary – Persephone was accorded every courtesy. The relevant 'missing persons' files from the period, miraculously retained, now on microfiche, but not destined for computer, did in fact have a distressingly meagre sheaf on

134

one, 'Jeanne (misspelt) Armour, Nurse's Aide'. Nothing at all on an 'Amelie Sanderson'.

So someone *had* reported the disappearance, and since the only civilian statement in the file was from a Red Cross matron, in late November, 1945, presumably it was the latter or the rehab centre. The statement, from one, Beatrice Thompson, tersely recounted a complained-of bout with a 'not infrequent' hospital infection, followed by Amelie's sudden absence. There had been no note or message to the world of any kind, no statements from any possible friends or colleagues. No relative or relatives were mentioned, either as existing or as having made inquiries. *'She was independent-spirited though...'*, and that comment, Persephone opined to James, she suspected may have sapped investigative zeal.

Only one other individual entered the record, in the person of a 'Tom Gunnerson' (misspelt), a private in a Canadian Pioneer battalion on loan to the British military construction unit out at Cairnryan. Persephone read James a sergeant's notation: *The male attended the Red Cross facilities, presenting himself as a friend of the missing woman, and asked for her. He was thereupon questioned by staff at the facility, and subsequently at the station by myself, and later released as not being considered a person of interest.*

Persephone folded her minimal notes and looked disconsolately over her glass. "Maybe I put too much stock in a fresh look at old material... now I'm thinking if we're to get *any*where, we'll have to find a living human being with a memory *and* some actual contact with her..."

135

To which James had to relate how *his* naive hopes after the sprightly Margaret's interview had been dashed by learning of her recent demise. But there *was* the gallery.

"Take a snoop at these, Seph, my humble line-up for you," and James flicked his iPhone to the snaps he'd taken at the Trust. "Whoops, hold it. My poor tech savvy," and he forwarded the snaps to Persephone's iPad for better enlargement.

"Hmm... possibly, no, nothing... faint likeness, nothing to go on really..." But the shot of the very young aide and the man in the wheelchair made her gasp slightly. "Dead ringer for my mam – can you believe it, even so young, and *so* long ago! Well done, Watson!"

The speculation about needing a live witness became clear when they realized the 'ringer' effectively meant nothing unless corroborated by the wheelchair occupant, *and*, that person had some traceable recollection to pursue.

Persephone propped James' iPad against the vinegar bottle and stared at it while slowly draining her lager. "In case you think me sloppy, I should assure, my dear fledgling colleague, I have also scoured, legally and not-so, every UK phone listing, missing person file repository, voters' list, newspaper archive, published wedding or death notice, etc., going back to immediate post-war, for Amelie Sanderson or Jean Armour, or combo of each."

"And?" James said, supportively.

"Zero Amelie S., zero Amelie Armour... lots of Jean Armours, not surprisingly – a baby-factory of a heritage namesake to be sure – but all either too old, still young, or dead with touching obits ruling out my aunt. A few Jean

Sandersons popped up: one, you'll be thrilled to learn, currently the first self-declared lesbian all-Scotland tennis champ, the several others were living students, a deceased and divorced family solicitor, an SNP flamethrower defrocked for sleeping with her daughter's boyfriend after a rally, and, well, just dead ends…"

"Take heart, Seph… we've barely started. Much yet to explore, I have a gut feeling. A tip suggests we attend the Stranraer memorial service tomorrow – talk about potential vertical observers from the past! C'mon, another round. I'm not driving…"

Persephone grinned bravely, then relapsed into her funk.

"And of course, the entire search is compromised by simply acknowledging that Amelie, if surviving the forties, may well have left the UK, and/or married and changed names, or, just plain gone underground in some banal scenario or place where she never had to use either of her names."

"That's it," counselled James, "back to the inn, and a bracing walk up to that great view of the sea the landlord recommended – you leading of course… love walking behind you, so inspiring."

16

They carry back bright to the coiner the mintage of man,
The lads that will die in their glory and never be old
A. E. H.

November 11, 2016, 10:30 a.m.

"My dad would be so tickled that I showed up for this,"
Persephone remarked out of the blue as they drove in to
Stranraer's rendition of Remembrance Day.

They parked a block away from the Sheriff Court and
Justice of the Peace Court, and joined a crowd
congregating in a steady drizzle. The cenotaph fronting the
halls of public accountability consisted of a Creetown
granite square pedestal supporting a bronze, Royal Scots
Fusilier.

For a hardened criminal lawyer, James displayed a
converse sentiment on such occasions. His congenital
affinity for voices from the past left him vulnerable to
sometimes uncontrollable tearing up, despite complete
lack of any connection to the event commemorated. As
well, it seemed profoundly unfair the day should be rained
upon.

"James, you softy," teased Persephone.

By ten forty-five, a crowd of close to 300 or so had
formed in widening semicircles before the memorial.

From a side street, four pipers and two drummers in full military tartans skirled and beat their way up to the foot of the silent Fusilier, accompanied by the sun bursting through. They followed the march with a classic melody of retreat, *The Green Hills of Tyrol*, then fell silent themselves.

A robed cleric, straight from BBC central casting, emerged to mount a small podium. He was stout, with wiry salt and pepper hair, rheumy eyes that gazed into the hereafter, and a square jaw, resolute in the face of perpetual human folly.

A greeting, a prayer, an adorable child reciting, flawlessly, *Flanders Fields*, then it was eleven and the awful, always disquieting moment of silence. That ended with the cleric's stage cough, whereupon, to everyone's total excitement and surprise, an original Hurricane and Spitfire thundered past one after the other, not 200 feet directly overhead. Despite the solemnity of the occasion, there was a ripple of spontaneous applause.

The cleric, who was admirably unaffected, resumed:

"This year, as the wreaths are laid, we recognize a special member of our community – and he's been a welcome contributor ever since he landed, if I may use that word – he was a Polish flier in our RAF, and at the age of twenty, the recipient of a DFC. We are indeed honoured and fortunate to have Group Captain Jan Rekawek here to lay the first wreath today."

A wheelchair rolled out from the front row, pushed by a woman in the 'Bluebirds' nursing attire of WWI; but then, to the crowd's mute respect, its bent, yet still lanky occupant stood, and walked shakily under his own steam to the memorial. A current RAF Flight Sergeant handed him a wreath entwined with red and white ribbons inscribed in Polish.

James stood rooted in his usual awe with such formalities. Whether or not there was gold to be mined somewhere in this event for the Amelie mystery, he was damn well going to offer this inspiring survivor a dram, a pint, a heartfelt thanks…

The veteran carefully laid his wreath with hands that shook, James thought, more from the significance of the moment than any palsy. He stepped back and saluted for a long minute, then turned and made his way back to the wheelchair. His 'Bluebird' kissed him on both cheeks which moved him to remain standing.

A local children's choir did a fine job with *O God, our help in ages past*, followed by a Korean War vet in navy blazer loaded with gongs, promising that, "*At the going down of the sun, and in the morning we will remember them.*" And then it was over, the pipers retreated gloriously, and James, followed by Persephone, made a beeline for the old flier as he settled into his chair amidst a gaggle of youngsters.

"Sir, I'm a foreigner like you were, and I've landed here to stay too. It would be a privilege to stand you to a drink today. Would you join us? Your escort here is welcome of course, and we'll see you safe home after…?"

The Group Captain's eyes fairly gleamed. His smile showed amazingly white teeth as he looked squarely at James.

"I'm your man, sir."

The Grapes

The escort quickly found comrades in the pub and was soon occupied at the bar. James steered their guest to a corner booth.

"It's not often you get to speak with someone who took part in such… um, *tumultuous* times – hope you won't think we're interrogating you!" With every intent of doing just that.

Three ales arrived and directly there was grateful froth on the airman's upper lip.

"Not at all, not at all, always good for me to talk with someone new… I'm ninety-one now, but my mind can still fly!"

"Guess you've seen a few of these ceremonies, sir?" Persephone began.

"Call me Jan, please – otherwise I might order you into a cockpit – seen too many of them maybe, and yet… they always shake up the memory. People, lost friends, come marching back again, just when they were almost forgotten – *but,* you know, there are some who *never* leave. At the end of the War, when I was a mess, recovering from burns and everything broken, I was cared for by such wonderful people…"

You could almost hear James and Persephone bite their tongues in unison; this was territory they'd hoped to wander into.

"Anyone in particular, or special, that stands out still today?"

"My wingco. Came all the way over from Londonderry just to make sure he could still laugh at my English… ha! And… and, *oh!* Yes, a young nurse volunteer, can't forget her, fussed over me like her brother. Used to read Scottish adventures and poetry to me when I couldn't walk…"

The two interrogators couldn't extract their devices fast enough. It was too Dickensian, as Persephone had admitted earlier, the wished-for coincidence, surely. She held her iPad up first, placing it gently below Jan's gaze.

"Could this be the girl you're speaking of?"

"My God! Yes, *yes!* Recognize her anywhere – wh-where – oh, the years…" and the old eagle clutched the iPad with both hands, his eyes visibly filling. You could almost hear the thunder of engines, screams, laughter, the bustle of crisp skirts, the soft and cheery words flying through his mind.

His rapt audience tried not to press, but let him navigate the obviously emotional passage back and forth.

"Is she… is she alive…? Do *you* know where she is, how she's doing – and, and goodness, what makes *you* interested?"

Not the desired miracle answer, but a real and moving nexus by way of flesh.

"My aunt. Sh-she was, er, *is* my aunt," Persephone stuttered. "And *we* don't know if she's alive or dead, or what happened to her after the War…"

The trio exchanged a rapid series of bewildered, open-ended glances.

"She took my heart you know, Jeannie, left us all very suddenly with no words to anyone..."

"Please tell us anything you can recall from your relationship – *anything,*" Persephone implored, "if not too troubling."

"She had her demons I suspect, but kept anything personal locked up... there *was* a friend, a boy, young man, a lover maybe... I teased her when she was ill just before she disappeared that she was actually pregnant. Told her I was insanely jealous – which I was – but of course, I knew nothing of the truth of all that... she used to go out on weekends to Cairnryan. I knew that. She told me she had magic hikes there, could see over the sea; she was planning things – what was her word, 'escapades' – for her future."

"Well, at least we booked into the right location, Seph," James had to say.

There was a natural pause as Jan took some long pulls on his glass and meandered down old paths.

Almost as afterthought, James asked, "And the young man, the patient in the photo? He...?"

"He's the man you're drinking with... can't believe I ever looked like that," and he added, not angrily, "I should curse you both for bringing Jeannie back, and showing me how I've wilted!"

Jan had in fact an active appetite, and all were famished after the event outside and gnawing stabs into the past. They both realized they had all they were ever likely

143

to glean from their subject, so James and Persephone laid on a hearty shepherd's pie and more ale. The *Gemütlichkeit* did a number on some of his darkest reaches, and what followed was a fascinating purge of Jan's war in the air. His hosts were given a sometimes disjointed yet hair-raising insight on aerial combat and Polish profanity.

A Land Rover had been assigned to shepherd Jan for the day, and so Persephone and James merely accompanied him and the escort to the curb, shook his hand and hugged him, before he was eased on board. As the engine started, he slowly lowered his window, as if re-opening the screen of his memory.

"That fellow, whoever he was. I should say I saw him once – must have been a boyfriend I assumed – tallish lad with a haystack of blond hair, huge arms. Noticed them because I was feeble at the time myself, and he had an accent, not English. He came in the front door as I was being wheeled into the garden, and I clearly heard him ask for Jean. It was shortly after she'd gone, but I don't know what he said or did when he learned…"

"Ever see him again?" quizzed Persephone.

"Never. And I guess that's two of us forever sad… please tell me if you find anything?"

Persephone was both reserved and agitated on the short drive back to the inn. James, like a good partner, tried to steer the transition.

"Don't know what *you* think, guv, but that was a great start. For me anyway, a promising immersion in the local

scene and a bygone era – don't think failure's relevant yet;
we've only *begun* to unravel first threads…"

"Appreciated," the driver acknowledged glibly.

"I tell you," and James leaned back, genuinely
committed to his observation, "more and more, I get this
whisper, from who-knows-where, that our HQ at
Cairnryan, and some clever rummaging about, will
produce results. I'm not a nutbar, just have that sense,
Seph…"

As they pulled in, an elderly man was being helped
from a taxi, and ushered into the *Auld Cairn*.

"Look, Seph, another gent we can treat at the bar,"
James quipped. "Maybe he's a fly-boy too."

17

And I will love thee still, my dear,
Till a' the seas gang dry
R. Burns

November 29, 1945
South Ayrshire coast, 9:30 a.m.

Fog spread like a giant carpet over the Firth of Clyde below a sunny, clarion sky, casting a dramatic scene from which U-2540 approached her execution chamber. Much like a reluctant pet ducking and tugging on a leash, His Majesty's battle-class destroyer, *Barfleur*, slowly extracted the sub from the grey shrouds through steely waters to within a half-kilometre of Ailsa Craig's eastern face, then shed her towlines.

Two to three hundred souls had risen early on a chilly morning to line the shore, curious to watch the killer's swan dive. Thomas Gunnarsson stood in a back corner of the chatty crowd. He'd hitched a lift with a couple from Stranraer who'd lost a son in the Murmansk run.

Though rolling, the sea sat relatively calm, and the doomed craft more or less rode the swell where she'd been set adrift, while its escort continued another kilometre north and laid off. Her bow swung slowly back round to face U-2540. About five minutes later, *Barfleur*'s forward guns flashed, and two seconds later, roared.

Like a tennis match, everyone's eyes shot downstream to see the result; the return volley consisted of a muffled thump, followed by a massive eruption of black smoke and towering flame. Several seconds passed before an even more thunderous eruption rocked the sub as well as the entire atmosphere. The inlaid munitions had performed their *coup de grace* efficiently; a second volley would be unnecessary.

A lone piper in kilt and a WWI tunic swung in with *Wild Mountain Thyme*, gauging his tune cleverly so that many in the crowd chimed in with *"And we'll all go together"* as the sub's few floating remnants surrendered, and were sucked below.

Children dashed about, understandably thrilled by the ultimate game played out for real before their eyes. Thomas stood impassively during the spectacle; he saw nothing joyous in the moment. His war had ended in utter, inconceivable loss. The best, and last, he could do today was gaze on his last connection with it – and so, as he saw it, the sinking of his heart.

***

Cairnryan, 2016
November 11, 6:30 p.m.

The post-Remembrance evening was just what the doctor ordered. Persephone easily charmed Connor, the septuagenarian host and bartender, and Mairi, his spouse and chef. Connor pulled perfect pre-dinner pints and cheerfully drew them into surrounding conversations.

The number of patrons in the tiny pub fostered conviviality across a spectrum of characters: an Edinburgh woman in her early forties, a pharmaceutical rep returning from routine rounds in Northern Ireland; an elderly couple from Armagh, whose forbears fled to Galloway temporarily to escape the great famine – the husband instructed James on the anomaly of the resultant 'Belfast Scots' and 'Galloway Irish' vernacular. And tossing a wild twist on the several accents in the room, a young couple from Georgia breezed in, full of 'y'alls' and gregarious smiles. James couldn't resist asking how they'd landed on the inn.

"Yessir! Saw y'all this mornin' at the ceremony – how we came here? Mah pa-*ternal* grandpa was an assault boat skipper at Normandy. Blown to pieces on Omaha. After D-Day, his letters from heah came back raving about Loch Ryan and its folks. Swore he'd return. Seems he trained in the area, practised landings on local beaches. Mah daddy died young, so it's us who comes…"

Rounding out the travellers were the older man seen earlier arriving at the inn, who spoke little but seemed to have a rapport with Mairi, and a youngish law professor from Surrey, recently divorced and "keen just to lose myself in the heather for a while". Connor gravitated towards James and the Southerner when he heard the War mentioned.

"If it's history grabs you, bide a wee second," he said, before disappearing behind the bar and resurfacing with a stack of local heritage journals and magazines. "Nineteen forty-four, forty-five, the loch was jumping with Canadian loggers, Yanks, Anzacs, all kinds of naval and military doings. There was a military port in town, blew up in a strange explosion in forty-five or forty-six – can't recall exactly – huge piers and docks right out in front of our place too. There's photos of them in some of these, must have been taken from our windows or close by, before we took over, mind. Pics of captured Germans too, marching right past here... help yourself, great way to drop off to sleep! And don't overlook the maps and trails..."

Georgia hesitated for a moment and was lost, as James scooped the meatiest-looking mags and those with promising photos, especially the one showing U-boats moored side by side at the Cairnryan piers at the end of the War.

18

Persephone awoke, as ever, in full throttle, determined to canvass the inhabited reaches of Cairnryan, door to door, in a contemporary dragnet – 'have you seen…?' – willing herself to uncover any new trace, a distant recollection, a scrap of departing rationale, *anything* to put her emotional, albeit self-imposed duty to rest.

Both found themselves eager to be outdoors, but James, who always went with impulse and instinct, chose to avoid humanity and prowl the local topography by taking all the likely walks and trails that might, if only by sheer continued existence, suggest a clue, a hint, physical *or* metaphysical. Hardly standard ops, but Cub Detective James hadn't done badly so far…

"Meet you at low tide in front of the *Auld Cairn* James. You're an old salt, can figure what time that is, and, I'll have a bottle of Linkwood with me – because we'll be toasting your discoveries."

Jesus! She really thinks I can produce…

"Aye, guv! But not to forget *your* superior skills. 'Fortune favours the shapely', or however it goes…"

"Bastard!"

Persephone was nothing if not diligent. She set out knocking and ringing on the weathered portals dotting Cairnryan's seaboard, beginning with the very first, tiny cottage after the *Merchant's House*, by late afternoon having exhausted both directions from their inn, including the expansive, stonewall-ringed Wallace estate, boasting white cannon at the gates.

She was hampered by natural distraction. The doors and structures were often classically quaint and colourful, the exterior age confounded either by a brilliantly modernized yet atmospheric interior, or simply a rustic throwback to wandering sailors and lonely wives, and she couldn't help enjoying her tour, but sensed, professionally, her efforts would prove futile.

"Morning, madam. We're making enquiries about a very old case, but would appreciate any memory or information you..."

Some responses from longtime residents were, not surprisingly, clouded: "But, dearie, I was just a wee bairn ye ken..." Amongst the very aged but still lucid, some verged on teasing. "There were so many comin' and goin' back then, an' the world upside down... sure there was young girls about, aye, but so were soldiers... just can't remember any particular lass, or young couple..."

***

James cheekily classified his morning sortie for himself as a *grand démarche*, to stoke purpose and zeal; it led him directly west from the inn, along the loch's north shore and A77, the sole road. As ever, the salt tang bit as he came even with the massive contemporary dockage for the Stena Line ferries. One was in port at that moment, gulls fussing at her stern, and James felt a reflexive twinge to just embark – but, he *was* a man on a mission.

He couldn't just step inside a long-ago young woman's psyche, but tried nevertheless to imagine what might have pulled her on board – though, in 1945, it would have likely been from back at Stranraer.

The 'Irish Sea': a romantic ring, yet he had to admit all he really knew was that countless wretches had crossed it in hunger and hope, and usually from the opposite direction. He pondered *their* passage more than any conviction something tangible might materialize on Amelie's fate.

The A77 soon turned north, to the right. James stood for a while at the turn-off and stared like a keen voyager along the continuing rugged coast. Deep blue and mauve glens marched into the distance, cleft down to the very water; their ridges rolled off in lush heathery greens, softening the rock cuts which James could see eventually dipping into the open ocean at the northwestern tip of the loch.

He plodded along like a good trouper for some time, thoroughly enjoying the venture, senses attuned for any speck or person that might prompt relevant speculation; however, while the terrain was edifying for the inner self, he was forced to concede it was uninstructive as to absconded aunts. Almost reluctantly, he turned round and began retracing his steps. A half mile or so on his way back, he noticed a small white signpost slanted into a rise above the road on the land side, now on his left, just outside the fringe properties of Cairnryan, obviously missed on his way out. Three upper crofts were inscribed in black letters, one above the other: *Little Laight, Lairdshill*, and *Bonniebraes*; the signpost pointed up a steepish earthen lane.

If I were young, amorous, or just keen to get off on my own back in 1945, would I trek along the coast road, as I just did, with the piers and military crowding about, or squirrel myself above it all, survey the scene, plot my fantasies – or flight into obscurity? Little question, surely... so James took the 'high road', smiling because he'd always wanted to be able to say he'd done so.

It was November, but a cloudless sky and palpably warm sun washed everything spread out before him on the incline. At the outset, there were upward-rolling sheep pastures, with hundreds of skeptical dark eyes turning away from his advance in shaggy waves to far corners. Endless blackberry bushes twined both sides of the lane. The three whitewashed cottages sat snugly beside small burns, or were sheltered by great oaks. If only to satisfy his envy as to how long they'd flourished there, James approached their portals, one after the other; but on this day, no one responded – *don't blame you...*

The next level wound upwards through what he could only call 'magisterial' stands of fir, with careless grouse whisking across his path into needled thatches in the forest. And then the way opened broadly onto a thick, course-grassed summit. Cows shuffled here and there at will around the stones of an old foundation.

Literary and olfactory sense suddenly fused in James as he approached the ruins, with the recall, almost

153

verbatim, of a line from a long-forgotten Buchan tale: 'there was a dry aroma... the savour of stone and tile and ancient crumbling mortar'. What surely were the entrance steps remained, leading into the airy past. James strode boldly up them to accept, graciously, a dram of the finest from the sure-to-have-been-winsome lady of the manse...

From the wrecked stoop, James peered far below and away to survey the loch spilling into the open ocean, appreciating the prospect from what had likely been either a porch or sitting room. He fooled himself he could just make out Ireland. One spot along the Chesapeake, and possibly Mont St Anne near Quebec City, flitted through his memory, but this vista was different. He felt uniquely 'up there', on a windy, silent, platform on the world. It demanded reflection, leeching cares and woes off into the blue expanse...

Amelie and the old flier's rival, surely they discovered this perch, cavorted, rejoiced here, made plans, and doubtless, loved up here – Seph needs to experience this.

A rumbling, congestive cough suddenly racked the air behind James, entirely discordant with his mood. He turned to see a male form slumped over, back against a large tree, perhaps ten metres away. The transparent fact the two of them were the sole interlopers in this lofty field prodded James to stroll over. His gesture seemed vindicated as he recognized the elderly gent first seen checking in the night before, and then later in a corner of the pub.

"Hello, sir. Everything OK?"

A candle flickered in the recesses of the misted, Baltic blue eyes, slowly illuminating James in front of him. The coughing yielded to a low whistle, then slowed to a strained breathing.

"No, no – oh, yes, I'm fine – just, you know, whacked out by the climb. Seems tougher…" and the deeply etched face looked directly at James, managing the ghost of a smile. "You're not from here too?" He was clearly flustered, almost disoriented. "Funny, spent my life outdoors. Now, gasping just to get up here…"

James refrained from the trite 'Come here often?', instead observing the equally obvious.

"Extraordinary, so expansive, peaceful…"

The man nodded without looking up either at the observer or the referenced scene. He appeared relatively calmed for the moment, settled amongst the needles and moss between the tree roots. James decided on a brief query, as politesse, and remained standing.

"Saw you in the pub the other evening. Stayed there before?"

Again, a slight nod with only tentative engagement.

"Uhm-m… yes, oh yes, many times – never leave really…"

No invitation to join his roost seemed forthcoming, and though there may well have been a fascinating life's tale to pry open, James had no expectation it would disclose the whereabouts of the errant Amelie. He leaned a little closer.

"Well, you're OK then," at which the old man merely blinked. "James, by the way…". No reply, so the 'man-on-the-hill' stayed nameless for the time being. "Take it easy, perhaps see you for a pint at the inn later?" and with that James wheeled off casually.

He looked back once before dropping below the summit. The fellow all but blended into the massive tree, with his grey sweater coat, grey sailor's toque, tan work trousers and boots. Widower? Loner on a favourite escape? Or, his budding author leaping to the fore, one from 'awa'', like himself, only years earlier? There'd not been enough discourse for James to detect an accent – *ha!* Ebenezer Balfour!

Maybe Seph's had some luck… and the pub was precisely the proper forum to determine that. Then he vaguely remembered 'low tide', and a 'bottle of *Ringworm*', or whatever it was…

19

Cairnryan
November, 1945

The Matron-Sergeant knew, directly after Amelie complained of nausea two mornings in a row. On the third such, she pulled the aide aside, sat her down and thrust a cuppa at her. Despite being one of the old school, she stated flatly, "Jean, you're pregnant. What shall we do? I won't be telling a soul, mind."

Recent illness had subverted specific bodily awareness: Amelie was thunderstruck. Love was on the menu; a child now was not. Not in her planned adventures on the high seas and wild mountain glens. Thomas was bonny enough but she sensed their youth would easily scare off any willingness for paternity. Inversely pragmatic to her fantasies, Amelie knew she was neither emotionally or financially ready to nurture. Family was not a warm concept in her experience, and what there was of it – Hortense – was in university, without time or means, let alone inclination to help out, especially now she thought of it, after her cold reception in Stranraer.

It wasn't shame or embarrassment; there were simply none about, close or caring, to be happy or outraged. Intuitively, Amelie understood it was just not her time. All this seemed clear, but she was nevertheless in turmoil from the sudden knowledge of the impending fact. A toll was taken.

"You look at least three months gone, Jean. Don't know how you missed it, but maybe being laid up with that infection hid it from us all. Be cautious child; you may be weakened," advice given to Amelie without knowing whether motherhood would be accepted by her or not. But then, shortly after, Amelie was gone, before the Matron could ever know.

A young body might have weathered events differently, but the lingering bacterial infection and an 'incomplete' miscarriage at twelve weeks left Amelie near-delirious. She didn't fully appreciate her true condition, despite 'cleaning up' best she could after the traumatic event, and felt horrifically alone as opposed to independent. As sepsis raced towards shock, she stumbled one evening from her windowless room in a forgettable bedsitter on the farthest reach of Cairnryan to which she'd fled, on a blurred mission to 'find Thomas'.

I should have told him... we could have... oh my heart... pounding, so fast...

Wild thoughts, stray recriminations, pure agony, all shot into the dark, starless sky as Amelie trudged up the steep path above the Old Coach Road. Only because they'd stolen there so often could she move robotically towards the upper pasture.

Is that a whale – no, a ship, steaming away down there? I should be on...

Amelie faltered, looked for a stone fence, but then, spotted 'their' tree.

158

He must be here, I feel he's close... I'll lie down till he finds me, just rest...

Far below, the second of the final three U-boats corralled in Loch Ryan glided out to her death off Bloody Foreland.

***

Late in the afternoon of a pensive yet liberating tour, James came on Persephone, seated – flopped, semi-fetal actually – in the grass above the sea wall bordering the inn. The sun, though still bright enough to catch her hair as a subtle beacon, was well on its way, loitering briefly above Loch Ryan's version of the Hesperides.

"Yo, dear guv."

The reclining DCI, in a funk, didn't look up.

"Zip. Nada. No *bludy* 'bingo!'..."

"You do look down, Seph. Testament to your efforts – but then, in despair, if I may, you resemble even more the Lady of Shalott..."

Luck clearly had avoided Persephone. She appeared all but resigned, on the verge of writing off any closure for her self-appointed family quest.

"Nice try, Sir James, but really... thrown myself on every old-timer's doorstep. Mickle wisps and creaks, but nae cries or whispers."

James, newly minted widower, spent some of his acquired resilience.

"Well Seph, that Limpwood you promised will come in handy. Not to make light of things, but from what I've seen today, we ought to raise a toast and smash the bow of whatever ship likely stole your dear aunt away…"

"'*Link*-wood' you *ijit*, and why are you sold on a sea exit?"

"… well, up on this hill today, I felt a pull, almost yearning, to head west, genuinely, out the gates as it were. Melodramatic, granted, but a powerful atmosphere, which, in my impeccable, *vast* investigative experience, compelled an inevitable sailing off – from *whatever* wretched or cogent circumstance."

James' superior officer sat up and stared at him, trying hard to maintain severity.

"And you think, because you're not a bad lover, and a partly reformed criminal brief, I should be mollified and bite the bullet?"

"Put it this way, I was thinking you might drive us, siren blaring, over to Port Patrick for supper. I hear that stretch of coast is a charmer."

It was quite late when they returned from a memorable feed on crab sandwiches at The Crown Hotel in Port Patrick. The *Merchant House* pub was by then closed, so James lost an opportunity to ply the old gent from the afternoon with the promised ale of remembrance. But they were well sozzled, and met sleep head-on.

20

November, 2016

Thomas Gunnarsson had served Trigony House, and its successive lairds and owners, well and faithfully, from private residence and shooting lodge into current hotel mode.

Over the decades, not a shrub, tree, rock path, clear-gurgling burn, wood structure, window, floor, table, chair, not to mention a mountain of split firewood, had escaped his strong and gentle hand. His once tall, robust frame was now bent with service, his Nordic features grown deeply creased and bronze, the soft blue eyes bathed in a watery sheen. Except for the absence – or perhaps *because* of the absence – of a consuming love interest, Hardy could not have drawn a more genuine character, beloved but reticent, firmly embedded in the local culture, far from the Dumfries crowd.

It had been nearly ten years since Thomas performed his appointed tasks, but the McDavid family had been loathe to simply cast him off. Instead, they nailed a wood plaque above his door, engraved, 'The Logger's' and over it, a pair of crossed flags: the Scottish griffin and the Canadian red maple leaf. His lair, his sole house in life, rent-free, till he parted, one way or another. His country of

161

origin was the single antecedent known to the good folks at Trigony, and Thomas had kept it that way.

Towards autumn's end the reclusive groundskeeper, now in his late eighties, woke one morning beneath a heavy blanket of lethargy: a sense that everything around him, his breakfast – lovingly delivered by the schoolgirl maid from the main house – his sacred tools, the future political alignment of Scotland, even his own longevity, no longer mattered.

A singular animus finally propped him up, dressed him in favourite work attire, stabbed his digits into the old rotary phone, and secured a week's potential stay at the *Auld Cairn*. He'd inexorably drifted back there for a weekend from time to time over the years, to be close, whenever an impenetrable fog of guilt or solitude descended; but today, there was a sudden, poignant urgency.

'Rory' McDavid, Trigony's current proprietor, accompanied 'old Armour' down the short lane to the estate entrance to see him onto the bus. He couldn't put a finger on it, but there was something almost ceremonial about their little procession.

"Out to Loch Ryan then, Thomas? Been a while, hasn't it?"

The keeper emeritus paused an instant, staring at the gravel.

"Aye," being his only Scottish assimilation. "Truth be known, sir, something in the air this morning, short of an actual voice, kept calling me…"

"You don't say! Well man, you were always one to heed the call, weren't you?"

Still, McDavid remembered this peculiarity for some time. It was entirely fitting to see Thomas disappear round the bend of A76 into a glen densely studded with giant firs.

***

For DCI Rodriguez, cold cases, especially her emotional venture into a murky family past, were not to be abandoned lightly. Liquor, laughter and wicked sex went a good distance to mute Persephone's urge to scream with frustration; but even so, a dense ennui, not unlike that recently experienced by the old man from Trigony dozing fitfully across the hall at the *Auld Cairn,* enveloped her the morning after Port Patrick. She didn't know what to proclaim; indeed, didn't want to *have* to proclaim any finality, when her mobile vibrated with a court-related crisis back at Dumfries. She rolled over and tweaked James' heavily purring nose.

"Right then, dear guv-in-training. Seems my evidentiary brilliance is unexpectedly required in the dock, but we're booked here two more days, and we'll no quit yet. Lounge here as long as you dare, I'll be back by dinner. Maybe you'll pull a miracle from the sky when ye're 'oot 'n aboot', Jamie, mine..." By which time she'd already slipped on a skirt-suit uniform and was standing at the door, car keys in hand.

Four different single malts had worked their kilted wiles. James thought he demurred well to Seph's sudden bustle by nodding empathetically and wafting a kiss; in reality, he grunted and nearly fell off the bed. When he stirred to the vertical around ten a.m., and focused roughly on how he'd been left solo for the day, his agenda stared at him less foggily.

An off day, but James would make it productive. Grab a fat sandwich and pint from the inn, a pen and papyrus, and climb back to that inspiring prospect. The sun was out, and he couldn't imagine a finer venue for scrawling on his generational opus.

It was, as any worthy author might have observed, an 'auspicious' morning – rather, *mid*day – as James, full of zest and well stocked with goodies, including a jaunty Kirkpatrick scarf, literally strode out upon the prior day's route, pleased with the minimal sun and crisp air.

There was the tilted road sign with quaint cottage names, the lane mounting through pasture and sheep, the latter now appearing, at least to James, less disgusted with his passing. By the time he'd skittered several grouse from his way, opened *and* closed ('PLEASE') somebody's gate and approached the summit, he was deep in plot machination and brilliant phrasing.

Brilliance suffered a minor jolt when the first object spied as he came over the rise was the old fellow from the day before. This time he was already seated against the same formidable tree. Despite his lingering curiosity, James opted for a cheerful wave and kept moving, selfishly preserving an uncrowded view for his creative frame of mind.

And it was a stellar literary afternoon indeed: five – *five* pages of deathless prose, barely discernible through scratch-outs, lines and arrows travelling in all directions, and numerous 'code' words to direct future emendation. At four p.m., James packed away his pen and paper, convinced he was finally in gear with a viable tale imbued with the violent, brusque colours of the clans. He stood slowly, inhaling deeply with a prolonged burst of sun before it chose to burnish the southeast shore in retreat.

A pleasant amble downhill, reconvene with his beguiling nymph, then plot the future with whisky of choice. The Amelie mission had, albeit reluctantly, all but dissolved in the dim mists.

The old gentleman although I pressed him hard would take no money, and he gave me an old bonnet for my head
R. L. S., *Kidnapped*

Mulling over the day's output, James sauntered right past the rust-grey head clapped in mottled hands, slumped against the sentinel tree. But a rasping plea pulled him back, and instinct made James advert with more than mere politeness. Hard though it was to imagine, it appeared much as if the fellow hadn't stirred since noon; on this occasion, however, he wasn't looking downward, but directly into James' eyes, as if importuning.

"You were… very kind the other day. Sorry I missed your beer… like a good pint, aye…"

"A problem easily rectified, sir…" James began, but the man reverted instantly to another wavelength.

"I ask your ear, 'favour' I guess it is. Need to tell someone, something I never told anyone. Learned to live with it, but can't now. Confession you could say, and have to make it today, here, now – *oh*, but not a murderer, no, *never*! I was so young…" and he looked off, as any elder might. "Been so alone, with her, with this. So empty, the years…"

James felt his feet drop anchor. Riveted, his only option was to collapse into a seat on the spot: the word 'her' had sounded a klaxon. How did these moments happen to him? *Could this be the one! Don't rush it buster…*

"You have a special… memory from this place?" James saw a tear squeeze from the old man's eyes.

"Memory, yes, so many… the morning I found her, here," and he unconsciously patted the turf around him. "She was sleeping – *looked* like she was sleeping – against this tree… *Oh!* But she wasn't. She was – there was dried blood on her legs…"

James didn't know whether to take notes for the trial or just sit like a spellbound kid at the storyteller's knees.

"There was no wound or other sign on her, and I hadn't known she'd been pregnant, but I assumed… two lives lost on this hill," and James saw an unborn child in the man's flooded eyes. He quickly perceived the human arithmetic was really three.

"I'll never know if something just went wrong with some butcher, or she feared her body, or, or society, and

166

did herself harm, or... I didn't know what to do, what was right. Tell the police and be charged – they'd already questioned me – how'd I found her body... her family would think I... But I couldn't leave her all alone up here. She'd come because of us, I'll never doubt that... and, and you know, she deserved a *military* funeral fair enough..."

James tried to loosen the atmosphere.

"Military? When was all this, sir? What brought you to the area?"

"Hmm? Ah, yes, the War, Second War. I was a soldier – yes, a *soldier* – but, but too young to fight they said, so they had me work on the piers and military construction. At the end, they brought in enemy shipping and I was working on that, just down the hill..."

"And..." James pressed gently, "you found this woman, at the War's end?"

A spasm riddled the man's body, before his mind clung to a moment of vivid clarity.

"November 28, 1945..."

"That's, that's seventy-one years ago – how can you re...?"

"... the day before they sank the last German sub," and he lapsed into a fit of raspy, horrifying congestion. James leaned forward to help, but the fellow suddenly continued, as if prodded by an invisible hand.

"But I *did* do something, and my heart went with her. I came here, again and again, to ask her forgiveness... I loved that nurse more than I understood."

James was speechless. What was *he* to do? He wondered what more he could elicit. He wanted to shake the old man till the whole story fell out, but as he pondered some possible lines of query, the agonized raconteur sighed himself into a conclusion.

"Said too much, maybe, but I... feel *lighter*, so strange," and he fell silent as his eyes dropped shut in apparent peace.

Not your normal client interview, James mused. But the confessor was hardly about to flee, and would of course resurface for supper at the inn. James reckoned nothing further could be humanely dredged from him at the moment; and frankly, he could use some time to digest – though he couldn't wait to introduce Seph. So he got to his feet in something of a daze and quietly moved off on the homeward path.

'Military funeral', 'enemy shipping', and especially, 'that nurse' all tumbled about his mind during an agitated descent to the coast road.

Not until he reached the shoreline bench in front of the *Auld Cairn,* and stretched out to consider possible induction into the Detective Hall of Fame, did James realize he'd clear forgotten to ask who 'her' was. A *name* for God's sake! The clincher; though who else could fit the requisite scenario?

This mental jolt and a sideways glance at the loch launched an oblique image in his mind: a Viking funeral! *But no, c'mon, that melancholy figure would never have orchestrated such a scene! Nor escaped it for that matter...*

The notion of fire, however, reminded James the air about him on this late afternoon was not so coddling. He was on the verge of his inaugural Solway winter. A snifter of *Bunnahabhain* – touted by Connor – beckoned from the salt-slicked slate and rising tide at his feet. He laughed to himself: *anyone able to pronounce that malt obviously hasn't had any…*

21

Mairi loved that point in the evening when, all diners served, she could quietly emerge from the kitchen to survey the aftermath. She often sat down with guests if they were from some distance, or begged her to reveal how in the world she made pheasant dance with white wine and blackberries. Tonight, however, it was concern for another more than chef's pride that pulled her around the room with the query, 'Have ye by chance seen the old gent, the one usually seated in the corner there?'

When Mairi paused at Persephone and James' table, she was surprised to be met with equal and genuine concern. Following James' energetic, almost breathless detailing of his hilltop encounter – complete with abject *mea culpa* for failing to elicit a name – every emotional, investigative fibre of her being told Persephone Amelie had been found. *It has to be her: boyfriend, nurse, this area, time frame.* And James fully agreed. If, as seemed probable, she was dead, how had she died, and where was she buried? What transpired so long go?

The couple waited and debated through a fine meal, barely able to contain excitement at cornering the last person to see her aunt, and getting the last, best picture…

Mairi let an almost maternal dismay show.

"He doesn't drive, ye ken. Just goes for long walks round and aboot. In all the years he's never missed a dinner…"

So keyed up themselves, James *and* Persephone omitted asking their target's name.

James looked out on the passing tide and the moon shooting icicles across Loch Ryan. It was colder tonight, even inside the *Merchant's House*. But he abruptly accepted the only course of action.

"Seph, we're getting our jackets, and make sure you bring your mobile – we're going to work off this feast."

"James! What… we're *wait –"*

"Exactly where we're headed. Mairi, thanks for an exceptional meal. Not to worry, we'll let you know."

Persephone was mystified, but James did indeed know exactly where they were headed, and, dare he think it, exactly what waited for them. He shivered.

Mairi too, was mystified, but pleased that someone was on the case. So keen were the couple, she waved off the bill: 'settle later over a whisky'. And the pair were off out the ancient door into a chilly darkness.

The still air of the speechless night
When lovers crown their vows
A. E. Housman

It wasn't how James planned to show Seph his idyllic writer's desk overlooking the loch. As they turned at the signpost for the three upper crofts, he felt his arm suddenly clutched, and not for warmth.

171

"Jamie, why do I feel a kind of dread – and not excitement?"

Because your intuition is razor sharp, dearest Inspector. But James tried to appear sanguine.

"Bet he's still up there. Don't know what I was thinking; he looked distinctly pekid, bit of a lost soul. Should've offered to help him…"

James was not a great believer in portents or ill omens, but they veritably clustered about him this evening. To the left, sheep in the moonlight floated like mini cotton clouds above a dark sea of pasture. When they reached the forest tier, towering black trees rose like ominous hands cupping both sides of the silver aperture to the upper field…

One of James' favourite art films was a sixties gem called *Blow-Up*, in which a London society photographer, prowling a park at night, accidentally records a murder. Back in his Chelsea studio, he develops a sequence of ever-closer shots of the same tree, looming in moody shadow and moon glimpses, which gradually plant an inescapable suspicion. James chided himself for allowing the suggestive parallel at this particular moment, but every bone in his body said it was germane.

When they broke onto the high meadow in nervous silence, James and Persephone immediately observed what James knew they would: the old man still slumped against the great oak. Like Rip Van Winkle, James hoped…

"He's sound asleep, must be frozen," ventured James as they halted at the protruding feet of the still form.

"He's stone dead, and does feel frozen," whispered Persephone, having instinctively leaned over to feel for a pulse. Even as she pulled out her mobile, Persephone was racked by contrary emotion: the urge to scream because now there would be no closure, besides death itself, from this person; and, whoever he might be, or was, sadness at a lonely end.

It took an ambulance and squad car a bare sixteen minutes to make it from Cairnryan to the fatal tree. In that interval, the two searchers reluctantly acknowledged their investigation had now been stymied.

Persephone paced in circles, exclaiming to a crystal sky, "It's like a bad movie, the key hook silenced at the very end, and everyone pissed at being duped."

"Nothing you could do, Seph," James added softly, "maybe, forgive me, the great scheme of things is simply admonishing us that a tormented soul – tormented *souls* – wish to sleep without further disturbance?"

Persephone looked forlornly into James' face.

"Aren't *you* enmeshed with your characters, dear James? Bless you for offering solace though," whereupon she tossed her hair to one side. "But no, my aunt, our women's line, what we know of her, all say no. Not go 'gentle into the night', or whatever; there should be *some* memorial of her passage, her passing."

Notes, diagrams, and photos taken, two medics rolled their night's find 'gentle' into *his* long night: his extended form barely fit into the black bag, then rear doors of the ambulance were shut. The local DS, no spring chicken himself, but a compassionate being for all the woe he'd attended over the years, approached the couple with great deference.

"Well, guv, none of my affair, but I understand there may be some connection here for you which is an unhappy one. Let me say I'm sorry for that; if anything we can do, please don't hesitate…"

"Na, na, not at all, Sergeant. You and your lot have been wonderful… truly."

"If it's any consolation, and no doubt you observed yourself, there seems nae sinister here. No wounds or marks, just an old jock who met his moment and went…"

Everyone shook hands, with contacts exchanged for any possible follow-up, and the sergeant's request they speak to Mairi, then the little entourage bumped off downhill, James and Persephone having declined a lift, choosing a mourner's walk to process the incident. Before leaving, James took a final, intense look at the tree which had played much in his recent hours.

"Seph, look at this. Didn't notice before… obviously, his body blocked it."

Its location made it ineluctably relevant, given two people originally implicated, an almost 'dying declaration' of love, and the gleaming fact that the most discernible of the two sets of initials carved beneath what remained of two hearts intertwined, was 'J. A.'

"Seph, *corroboration*, from a long-ago knife!"

A slight smile, perhaps of distant kinship, crept over Persephone's face.

"Heartwarming and pathetic at the same time I suppose… can't quite peg the first set though, 'J' or 'T', and 'G', or 'J' or 'T', and 'C', but that's our bloke, and Mairi, if only from the register, should easily resolve that."

Despite the apparent finality of circumstances, James suddenly felt even more reason not to throw in the towel.

"Police records and obits gave us nothing – and really, why would they, from what you know of her – but what about cemeteries? Now we're virtually certain 'her' is Jean and she was dead back then, why not do a tour? Forgive me, but she didn't just rot here. There's two, I believe, around Cairnryan."

They were almost at the signpost as Persephone turned abruptly and exclaimed, "You'll make a copper yet," then surprisingly, she laughed, "no, wait, let me beat you to it, 'you *have* made a copper', and she quite loves you – but you're on to something. *Cemeteries*. Assuming we learn his domicile, maybe there's a will lurking about, and maybe it directs where he's to be buried? A fellow that eternally smitten, dying under 'their' tree, surely he'd want to lie beside her?"

Or maybe he *was* lying beside her, but James didn't want to pursue that now.

Arms meshed naturally behind their backs as the two mourners quickened pace back to the inn.

22

Mairi was all ears and emotion when James and Persephone returned. In fact, she was waiting on the front stoop; police cars with siren screaming and ambulance trailing didn't tear past her placid outpost on the loch every night. Genuine tears leaked down ruddy cheeks when she heard the essential news – though her two volunteer searchers didn't share Persephone's personal stake in the affair, especially as a glimmer of further clarification still lingered.

"Such a quiet gent, so soft-spoken and polite... seemed to have a deep connection of some sort with our piece of the earth. Came many times over the years, would go on treks by himself – I packed lunches for him, aye – sometimes he'd even come into the kitchen and help with the dishes after dinner..."

Mairi got up hot tea and whisky for the three of them despite her sadness.

"He said something once which made me wonder if he'd been here, or near here, during the War, but I never pushed the poor man on it."

As promised the sergeant, Persephone began to advise Mairi to lock the man's door, thus allowing local police until the morning to check out personal or material items, but shrieked as she heard herself say 'the man's...'

176

"Oh my God, we've done it again, Jamie! His name, his *name* for Christ's sake!"

Mairi didn't hesitate.

"Mr Armour of course, aye! Jean Armour. And ye ken, he always signed it with 'Esq.' at the end, because, he told me, 'it sounds more weighty, and some people assume I'm a woman…'"

The two guests were momentarily stunned. Mairi got up and cleared the cups and saucers.

"Then who is 'T…', etc.? Not another for Pete's sake, not a rival surely, and he pulls a Tom Dooley up there and…?" spluttered James, barely able to wait for their host to disappear into the kitchen.

His partner was on it directly though.

"Na, na. Nae worry, luv. That's Jean Armour we found up there, and it was Jean Armour *he* found up there all those years ago. Like I said, one so smitten, bit of a loner… she changed her name, why shouldn't *he?* A gesture of pure fidelity. And let's face it, took his name, whatever it originally was, out of the limelight in a way."

James took a minute to swallow his perplexity, then bowed his head.

"Knock me out, Seph. You processed what's known, I chased unsupported whims."

Mairi blew them a kiss of gratitude as the pair went up the twisting stairs to their four-poster in something of a deflated mood: been quite the day. They entered their room and both automatically went to the window with the view west down the loch and out to sea. After a minute or

177

two gazing, Persephone pronounced the now-evident requiem.

"Well, we know she never did sail awa'," she said, and after another minute of reflection added, "and their might have been a cousin, elderly at that, for me…"

James gave her a promising hug, but she slipped quickly under the duvet.

"Sorting the years and tears, laddie… come the morrow, I'll wreck your bones," and with that she fell instantly asleep.

It was twenty minutes before it dawned on James that Amelie might well have 'sailed awa'' after all – though in unusual fashion.

Restless, both from the day's revelations and the circle untidily closed, James lay awake thumbing the local history magazines Connor gave him till he found the issue with the article on captured U-boats dragged in to Loch Ryan. There were several photos: one, eerily looking as if it had been taken from their bedroom window, showed German officers and crew assembled on the deck of a U-boat moored at the now defunct pier at Cairnryan. The caption read: *November 27, 1945. U-2540, last of the subs towed into Loch Ryan, sheds its captured crew before eventually being scuttled.*

James' eyelids were fluttering as he attempted the subsequent issue of the magazine, but his eyes widened when he scanned the 'Letters' section. A Hamish McNab, from Troon, had written in: '… *not 'eventually', but two days later. I remember because it was my birthday, Nov. 29, and the day began with me being taken by my parents to the shore at Girvan to watch U-2540 go down. And she wasn't scuttled, she was blown to smithereens by a British destroyer...'* The Editor's Note below the letter described the events of November 29, 1945 off Girvan's shore in much greater detail.

The magazines slid off the bed as James sat upright and words from the last two days flew spontaneously through his mind. *The tight cluster of dates!* The world of cold steel, salt and a distant wartime suddenly didn't seem so divorced from a young woman's fate on a high Scottish meadow.

And then, 'I *did* do something', 'military funeral', 'the day before they sank the last German sub'... he wouldn't just have lugged her off into some dirt behind a bush. Not the old man's character, and it didn't rationalize the need for 'forgiveness', surely – *oh Jesus! Oh yes, of course! Amazing...*

Macabre, yet arguably 'something' indeed done. A personal, secret, grand gesture by a frustrated young soldier and grieving lover.

In less than ten minutes, James had googled the tourism site for Girvan, discovered and noted departure times for the antique paddle-wheeler, *Waverley*, noted the location of a florist and a used book shop in Stranraer, then padded downstairs to leave a note at Mairi and Connor's door asking a bagged breakfast and a wake-up just before nine.

He drifted off like a kid anxious for Christmas morning, but woke briefly to email the florist that he had urgent need of a fine wreath with red roses, and would be there to pick it up around ten a.m.

23

Amelie Sanderson's faithful niece awoke with the terse resignation only a seasoned crime officer can muster. '*The past is another country*', or however it went; time to journey forward. She slunk out of bed and went to the window to look west down the loch once more. It glinted alternately in grey and chalk blue. The sun hadn't brushed the swells yet, but Persephone knew it would, and the future must now segue, quite naturally but joyously, to her 'American friend'. If he didn't propose something permanent, she would dangle him from the *Auld Bridge* and let the ducks peck at his feet till he swore to wear her tartan…

"*Yaah…!*"

"Morning, lass."

James materialized from behind with a soft hug.

"Get dressed, Inspector, we're off in a few minutes. To a ceremony I've presumed to arrange. I've commandeered your trusty roadster. Trust me… today, I think, I hope, you'll find a case truly closed and a soul found and celebrated – but please, don't ask me anything further right now. Hardly believe it myself."

Persephone was speechless. *What investigative wizard had washed up on Solway's coast* – or, had he lost his marbles and been swept back out with the morning's tide?

10:15 a.m.

The Stranraer florist had miraculously opened her email on arrival, and a thick-vined wreath, flush with glorious red roses, was waiting for James' credit card when he zipped in. They did have to wait a couple of minutes for the WHSmith manager to appear with his Americano and pasty, but James' initiative was rewarded: what self-respecting Scottish shop wouldn't guard a fine copy of *Treasure Island*? With illustrations by N. C. Wyeth no less!

Persephone, bewildered but compliant, agreed to inscribe the copy, and wrote, before leaving the shop, *for dear Aunt Amelie, and her own treasure island, love, Persephone.*

Had James found her grave? Where were they headed...?

"All right then, back through Cairnryan and up A77 and the Ayrshire coast, miss, if you will. Headed for the throbbing metropolis of Girvan, and we're right on schedule."

"Are you by any chance a demented Morse?"

But her passenger would only offer a grim smile and Mairi's bulging breakfast bags. The latter, and two Americanos of their own, occupied the first stretch of the drive, not to mention the wild, inspirational scenery.

181

'*Paddy's Milestone*', '*Creag Ealasid*', or '*Ailsa Craig*', as James Kirkpatrick first spied it on the map back in the *Globe,* endures as a perfect fantasy. The dramatically isolated appearance of its conical 240 acres, so near yet so far from land, pricks all but the dullest imagination.

Volcanic origins threw up jagged columnar rock to ring the island, leaving only the southeastern stretch accessible. At one end of that stretch, a great cave opens forty feet above the water, once found to harbour stone caskets with bones interred: a regular smuggler's idyll. And a small loch, of all things, twinkles some 810 feet up the same east side, seventeen feet deep.

Historically, Ailsa has never been consistently populated, though lying a mere ten kilometres off Girvan. It served in turn as way station for pirates on the Irish Sea, refuge for Catholics from the Reformation, and a three-storey castle meant to deter Philip II of Spain once crowned its eastern slope below the loch. A solitary tower survives today to guard the vestiges of a more recent granite quarry and mineral extraction enterprise. The occasional batch of unfortunates was imprisoned on the clump during the eighteenth and nineteenth centuries, and a lighthouse lingers from the 1880s, now automated. The true inhabitants continue to be myriad puffins and gannets, the latter hunted by Robbie Burns' maternal uncle for their 'succulent' flesh.

Had she ever set foot there, Amelie's dreams could never have been more colourfully realized.

182

It was Ailsa Craig which now confronted Persephone, still in her driver's seat, parked in Girvan's harbour, as James purchased two tickets for the *Waverley*. The rock sat hazily out on a proverbial azure sea. Were they about to sail out to meet a weathered seer to learn the rest of the story, or…?

"Grab the wreath and the book, Seph, she leaves in ten minutes."

It was a Monday, so they were two passengers amongst only ten or twelve others to board the *Waverley,* the world's last ocean-going paddlesteamer, for its late morning circuit out and around Ailsa Craig. The craft, and it richly deserved to be styled such, was a testament to the grace of a bygone era: long, low-gunnelled, sleek, much like a black and white seabird headed into the wind, with two red funnels in place of head crests. James, ever the nostalgia buff, easily imagined elegant women in long skirts and shawls being shepherded to better views along the deck by men in ermine-collared great coats.

Persephone gravitated directly to a forward railing, now only somewhat less bewildered, but anxious not to lose visual contact with whatever in the world awaited on this bizarre occasion. James caught that and did the right thing, which was to hasten directly to the saloon and procure two large hot chocolates with double rum injected. On his way back, he poked his head in briefly at the captain's wheelhouse.

Anticipation, and the liquid warmth, forced a winsome peek at James over the rim of her cup.

"Aye, ye're a devil, Sir James, enticing a wee girl tae the shores o' the insoluble! Ha' ye nae respeck for the daid?" she said, broguing up in a weak effort to glean more.

"On the contrary, Seph, be patient, had a word with the man upstairs; I'm confident all will be revealed shortly."

Which of course, as the *Waverley* steamed off from the pier, only mystified Persephone further: James had never struck her as in any way religious. She looked a bit like a self-conscious schoolgirl, standing in jeans and leather jacket, collar up, clutching the wreath and book, sipping her drink.

The day was indisputably brilliant in every sense: modest swell off the bow, a sparkling sun for late autumn, and the temperature just crisp enough to make the hot beverages perfectly justified. For a moment, James almost forgot the mission at hand as he watched a young lad race to the bow and launch his paper dart into the wind. It flashed in the sun, then immediately did a loop-the-loop and flew straight back to be mangled in the port-side paddle wheel. James smiled, filing the little diversion as a future metaphor of some sort.

Despite a mysterious agenda, the two arms of the law were comfortably entwined in the moment and their unplanned voyage, peering forward as the great rock drew nearer and Ailsa unwrapped her shades and mists. Above the shrieking gulls, the loudspeaker informed passengers of her history and legends. An older man, an obviously avid curler, delighted in explaining to a very tolerant spouse the granite extraction process once proudly situate on Ailsa's slopes.

The *Waverley*'s scheduled course circled the volcanic isle, and all angles were fascinating: on one side, mainly the Atlantic side extending round the southerly end, giant icicle-like crags rose treacherously, stacked together in the thousands, with a dark cave beneath one stretch, well above tide level. Coming back into waters visible from Girvan, the steep slopes gave the impression of being carpeted down from the summit in what James imagined were great swatches of green felt. Halfway down, but still literally towering, the sentinel from the old castle kept an eye below on the white buildings of the lighthouse and the abandoned rail tracks for the old quarry that ran along a protruding beach.

Persephone shed all other prospects for a moment and teased James with the proposition they should pack a champagne picnic some day and park themselves on the top peak, and just let the world float about them for a spell – and what would a whole night up there hold as an experience? James loved the idea…

Then the *Waverley* slowed her wheels to a silent glide and the loudspeaker intoned with a new voice.

"*Ladies and gentlemen, yes, this is the Captain speaking… during this month, we always make a special point of directing attention to the waters about 100 metres off our starboard bow even as I speak…*"

Persephone's head shot up and she looked into James' eyes. *This has to be it*, whatever 'it' was. James said nothing but smiled back knowingly, placing his finger on his lips.

"… *When hostilities ended in World War II, more than seventy survivors of Hitler's Rudeltaktik, better known as the Wolf Pack, surrendered, and were towed from the North Atlantic into Loch Ryan, just southeast of the Ayrshire coast. After their crews were marched off and the submarines examined by military intelligence, they were dragged back out to sea off Northern Ireland and scuttled. However, as perhaps a symbolic and dramatic finality, U-2540, the last of the corralled U-boats, was pulled from Loch Ryan to this very spot on November 29, 1945, set adrift, and a British destroyer standing off about a kilometre north, opened fire and sank her in a catclysmic explosion…*"

Every mobile passenger immediately rushed to the starboard to peer into the depths. As if a scrap of hull, a shred of uniform, or some relic would surface on demand.

But only James, of all the world still living, knew what actually lay below. He spoke very softly.

"Now, Seph, the wreath… and whatever you might wish to say, and then the book."

In a burst of emotion, Persephone hurled the vine and roses like a discus, a good five metres over the dark water. Bystanders on the deck looked askance, some even aghast, supposing audacious Nazi relatives had contrived to creep on board.

"Well done, Seph, now the book. She'll want it handy…"

The dutiful niece thumbed *Treasure Island* for several seconds and whispered, "You'll have a friend in Jim Hawkins, and... in case you didn't know, your lover's been supremely faithful..." before closing the book and managing to toss it within feet of the floating wreath. Onlookers continued flabbergasted.

All this Persephone executed without question on the strength of James' inspired initiative, and her thunderbolt perception of what had transpired so long ago. As he hugged her gently, James explained his rationale and 'supporting evidence' bit by bit.

For some time Persephone said nothing, occasionally nodding but kept her gaze over the water. Just when it occurred he'd maybe pushed things not really his domain, James fell victim to a devastating warm kiss, and a blessing: "You are unequivocally correct in every iota of your premise, and eternal kudos for not falling asleep when I did last night."

"Ah, then, has all this possibly been the start of a beautiful friendship, Inspector?"

"James Kirkpatrick, I'm arresting you for..."

Love took up the glass of Time and turn'd it in his glowing hands
Tennyson, *Locksley Hall*

"Ever seen or heard of *The Thin Man*?" asked James, hoping the wicked chemistry between Nick and Nora in the vintage detective films might inspire Persephone.

They were well on their way back to Dumfries, having left Mairi and Connor a fond farewell and a genuine promise to return, perhaps for New Year's, but for sure the following summer. They'd departed a night early feeling the inn wasn't, just for that intense moment, the place to linger in. The top was down, and James could see Persephone's breath as she smiled coyly and replied, without hesitation:

"Na, and hae ye nae seen *Granchester*?"

"Nope, so I suspect, touché?" He found it a real buzz when she burred.

"Aye, lad, and just to confirm, the *handsome* priest in that series can't help annoying the local, overworked Inspector, by assisting in crime detection…"

James laughed, joyously, for the first time in months, he realized.

"My great-grandmother would have said 'you're a caution'…"

"And I'm issuing *you* a caution, sir."

"To wit?" James yelled into a blast of wind.

"Get your hand off my knees or we'll plunge into the *Urr!*"

***

The rest of the way home, as James now happily accepted it, they tossed delicious conjecture back and forth whenever the wind allowed. The farther they put Cairnryan behind, the more the *fait accompli* of life together infused every burn, granite crag, wooded glen, and the open road, with fresh lustre. James felt giddy with the patent reality. He put his head back luxuriously and 'blethered on' as Seph listened, and toyed with finding a lay-by and fully exercising that term to consecrate the occasion.

"Here's an idea, Seph: me as your unpaid gofer, a hidden asset for Dumfries-Galloway law enforcement! On those rarest of occasions when you are stumped, and all about are losing their heads, there shall I be, ready and enabling, an unbiased but seasoned minion of the criminal mind, a prodder towards the grim truth. And all else failing, in deathless and snappy page-turners, I'll extoll your forensic wizardry – we can linger over those tales on Buchan evenings by the fire, single malts at hand – and of course, my gushing royalties will be invested in Sulwath Breweries…"

How was this New England sailor flung onto my shore! Persephone found herself blotting out the mundanity and random horror of her daily world, sensing she could suffer things more with a constant partner waiting – and what exquisite fate! Two lovers of language and antiquity, two 'bookies', two insouciant aficionados of the rule of law still tempered by compassion.

And, Seph, bless you, don't overlook the lovemaking and Scotch…

It was early evening when she dropped James off at the *Clog and Thistle.*

Christmas lights popped up here and there on their way into town, and copper and brief both knew this season would ring with special panache. James already wondered, *what do you get a classically educated detective chief inspector with one marriage in the past anyway?*

The driver looked her passenger straight in the eye as he extracted his bag from the boot.

"James, d'ye mind your family keep I introduced you to before our sortie to Cairnryan, and the auld kirk fronting the field and moat? And perhaps the rectory, the fine stone outbuilding? Can you *imagine* the creative mess we could make of the interior? Only a half-hour from Dumfries, yet in the best of country and plumped with history. Here's the thing, it's for sale – are you in, my James?"

***

James was packing up his few things after his final night at the B&B, musing on his recent vagabondage – *Seph'd have a field day with that word* – when Sheila Stubbs, his vivacious landlady, popped in to deliver an envelope. It was clear she would miss him. It was addressed to 'J. Kirkpatrick, c/o General Delivery, Dumfries, Scotland' and he wondered how in the world it had found him.

"Hope it's not HM's Revenue, or whatever you Yanks call it," teased Stubbs.

"Ha! Careful, ma'am, don't consider myself a doodle-dandy any more…"

"Ye're lucky my ex-partner's a Kilpatrick, and the old gent at the post office handed me it by mistake. *Anyhoo*, we'll look to see you again, in tartan, *haid tae foot!*" With that Stubbs bussed James quickly on one cheek and whisked off.

James confronted the envelope like it was a dead bird. There was no imprint or return address on the outside. Rather whimsically, he'd tossed all expectation of ever again receiving mail. He opened it slowly to find three printed pages, the second bearing a handwritten ink signature, the third being a photocopy of an email message. The letter was dated two weeks earlier, and bizarrely, came from an old adversary, the assistant DA for Portland County.

There'd been absolutely no love lost between James and Edward Grosvenor II, professional or otherwise. Awkwardly, their spouses had become friends via Charlie's gallery network, so every instinct cued James for some acid reflux from his abandoned legal haunts. He remained standing, eager to consume and discard the intrusive tentacle.

Dear James,

I hope this somehow finds you. I am so truly, helplessly sorry for what I have to say. We were never friends, only our wives, which makes this even sadder and more devastating, but I have to get my own words out, distinct from any other communication you may get.

Barbara often mentioned 'Charlie' in admiring terms, both cultural and physical, and I recall last spring she pestered me with attempts to get us all together sometime for an 'ice-breaker' dinner. You need to know Barbara suffered from a very severe form of bipolar disorder. In March, there was a brief passage in which she exhibited various degrees of delusion – psychotic, now things have been re-examined. She had gone off her meds at some point that month as I discovered, though in due course she levelled off.

*Three weeks ago, in purging stale messages from my home computer, I came on one obviously sent and read, though never by me, in late March; Barbara and I had mutual access to the home computer, and a joint personal email address. Given the location of Charlie's death and the nature of the discovered message, I had no option but to contact the police. The police, with full cooperation from me, determined that Charlie, in the elation of the moment on the day she died, sent you what was intended as a romantic message, but inadvertently pressed **our** address – most probably by reason of recent back and forth between herself and Barbara. In any event, Barbara read the message assuming it was in some response to her*

192

repeated invitations and drew a tragically wrong conclusion, then snapped. The email is enclosed.

Many years ago, I admitted a brief affair with a junior attorney, and we patched things up – but your own intelligence will tell you what pierced Barbara's mental fog on reading the message, and horribly, what happened next. All of that has been confirmed after re-interviewing the Press desk clerk, examining dry-cleaning records of the period, and rationalizing the absence of a common utensil from our kitchen.

The rest is chaos, for all of us. Barbara is charged with manslaughter, and who knows what may turn out; she has virtually no recall of events, and is an uncomprehending mess. We will not be continuing together. I have resigned from the D.A.'s office and have no future plans.

I so deeply appreciate your loss, and in some parallel way, I imagine I will undergo a similar grief. In whatever way, I hope you have found a new beginning, may comprehend my profound revulsion, and accept my sincerity in all this.

Ted Grosvenor

James now had to sit; he felt like he'd been reading for hours. The first two pages fluttered to the floor as he gripped the remaining email with both hands as if it weighed a ton.

From: Charlotte Kirkpatrick < charliekirk@hotmail.com>
Date: Friday, 27 March 2016
Subject: sex
To: Barbara Grosvenor < barted@gmail.com >

Dearest 'Heathcliff',
Let's celebrate! See you at the Press tonight, around 6 pm – you know the room.
xoxo Catherine

It was transitory, but James managed to salute Grosvenor's painful contrition, before simply staring at Charlie's email. It was, in the purest sense, a message, a loving one, from the great void.

James stood finally, and passed directly into the B&B's parlour where an early morning log fire crackled. Without any hesitation, he cremated the envelope, the three pages, and his past

***

As if they'd been an item for ages, Persephone knew exactly where to find James and when. At ten thirty a.m. she breezed into *Scrumptious*, and as she did the first time, immediately took an uninvited bite of his sacred scone, then quietly led him by the hand out the gate. And fittingly, he knew where she was leading him.

In a few minutes the pair leaned in perfect harmony over the stones of the Auld Bridge on a deliciously sunny morning, charmed by the river's gurgle as it slushed under the gathering ice and over the Caul. They hadn't exchanged a word since crossing White Sands and stepping onto the ancient trestle.

"Seph?"

"Such stillness. Nae need to say *muckle* this morning, is there?"

"True, true… and yet, I feel like I should consecrate these stones; they literally span my experience in Scotland…"

"Very clever."

James flicked a scone crumb from his upper lip and watched it land, stark against the bluish-white below.

"… couldn't help thinking what a waste of a brain, and a life, that Duncan boy inflicted on himself."

Persephone looked downstream towards the Edwardian footbridge, hiding a sly grin. "Well, my James, no child of ours would be allowed to stray from love like that."

The crisp air held the import squarely in front of James' eyes. He turned.

"Maybe it's time to let 'Rodriguez' slip into the Nith?"

An honest pause.

"Aye…"

"*So-o-o*. Maiden name? Could easily have chased it down, but never chose to."

The sun flashed off the thin sheets of fresh ice crinkling below.

"Kirkpatrick."

Author Note

I admit personal sentiment in sleuthing the backdrop for Dùn Phris. My full name is Christopher Kirkpatrick McNaught, and numerous of my direct forbears, William McNaught, Spirit Merchant included, who died at sixty in Dumfries in 1844, repose beneath St Michael's sod, not ten metres from Robbie.

Apart from centuries of serving locals fine, and I hope, undiluted whisky, and losing McNaught *émigrés* at sea, our Dumfries lot has evidently continued to 'give':

(Interior wall, St Michael's, Dumfries, for parishioners killed, *1914-18*)

James Kirkpatrick
Donald McNaught

(Exterior, St John's Scottish Episcopal Church, Dumfries, for those killed, *1939-45*)

Pte James McNaught
Pte Donald McNaught
Sgt. (W.D./A.C.) William J. D. McNaught
L. A. C. James McNaught
Pte J.J. Kirkpatrick D. C. M.
Pte James Kirkpatrick

(Town centre memorial, Kirkcudbright, *To The Glorious Dead, 1914-1918*)

Pte Peter McNaught, K. O. S. B.

May they sleep in honour unbetrayed
And we in faith and honour keep that peace, for which
they paid

9 781784 656492